BIG
MAN

WITHDRAWN
UTSA LIBRARIES

WITHDRAWN
UTSA LIBRARIES

BIG MAN

A NOVEL BY

Jay Neugeboren

Houghton Mifflin Company Boston
The Riverside Press Cambridge
1966

First Printing   R

Copyright © 1966 by Jay Neugeboren
All rights reserved including the right to
reproduce this book or parts thereof in any form
Library of Congress Catalog Card Number: 66–18108

Printed in the United States of America

for Betsey

PART ONE

ONE

I GOT no kicks coming, though. I live okay. I get up in the morning and my mother fixes my brother and my sister and me some breakfast. If my old man's up he eats with us too. Then I move my bones outside. Fat Julie's already there. How old is he now? Twenty-six? Twenty-seven? He just sits in his wheelchair with that stupid baseball cap on his head, reading sports magazines and comic books, making believe I don't exist. "Hey there, Julie," I say to him. "What's new in the world of sports?" He don't look up. He never forgives me for what I did. Who cares? Maybe he'll die soon. It's over five years and he still won't talk to me. What'd he expect? I wasn't no God, like in the magazines. These guys who spend their lives reading about ballplayers and worshipping them, they're full of it, you ask me. "See you tonight, Julie," I say. "Don't place no bad bets."

Then I go to work. Work is okay. I wash the cars and screw around with the guys to keep from going nuts, mess around with the women who come in. Sometimes that pays off. Then I come home, try to kill time. Sometimes I watch TV, sometimes I go for a walk with my brother up Flatbush Avenue, sometimes the Penguin calls and I go to his house, sometimes I just go to sleep. Who cares? The weekends are the only thing that matter. Then I go to the schoolyard. That's what I still live for, dumb me. Oh yeah. Don't even get to go every other weekend now, the glorious job I got. In the schoolyard they call me Plastic Man. "Hey, Plastic Man," they say when I walk through the gate. "How's it going, babe?" Oh yeah, you don't watch out, Mack, you gonna be dragging your body down to that schoolyard when you fifty, all these young kids running around you and through you and jumping over you, but they still gonna call you Plastic Man. Only you not gonna be stretching and sliding and leaping then. You gonna be wishing you could change yourself into a bench or a backboard, your rate.

All the lights are out in the living room. My old man sits in his rocking chair going back and forth. "C'mon, Jackie boy," he says. "You show 'em how, you mother." The Dodgers are playing the Giants and Jackie Robinson is dancing off first base the way he does, making the pitcher crazy. He fakes one way, then the other and the pitcher steps off the rubber. The TV men got the screen split so you can see Jackie on one half and the pitcher and batter on the other. Soon as the pitcher moves toward the plate Jackie takes off. "Move, Jack! Move, you bowlegged bastard!" my old man yells. The throw is right to the bag but Jack, he gets such a jump he's there before the ball, plows into the man at second like a football player. My old man comes over to me, punches me in the arm. "You see that, Mack? You see that? He's really something, that Jackie! How you like that —?"

He walks back and forth in front of me, mumbles to himself, I know he's not finished yet. "That guy gettin' up slow is Mr. Alvin 'Blackie' Dark — ain't that something? He's a southerner and he can't do nothing to Jackie!" He punches me in the arm again, then stops. "Hey, Mack — how come you think that is? Why you suppose a southern white man call himself Blackie?" He tosses his head back and laughs. "Ain't that something? When Jack gets too old to play and got gray hairs growing on his skull they gonna call him Whitey, I bet." I go into the kitchen and get a beer. My mother looks at me but she don't say nothing. I get back to the living room I'm just in time to see Campy drill the ball into left-center. Jack is off and running, my old man screaming at him, he crosses the plate standing up. "Didn't I tell you? Didn't I? For a bow-legged pigeon-toed old man he can still move, huh?" From the kitchen my mother yells to turn the set down and stop howling. She says my brother got to study. My brother's fifteen, goes to this special high school in New York, where he studies music. He's good. My old man turns down the TV and gets back in his rocking chair. I know what's coming next. "I always told you baseball was the sport," he says. "That's where the money is. I said so the first year Jackie come up. You know how much he makes a year? — over fifty thousand dollars, and that don't count the money from his book and the movie and things like baseball gloves." I get up and walk out with my beer. "I'm talking to you — I'm telling you something — !" he yells after me. It's better this way, walking out, otherwise he gets me too mad. I go to my room, sit down on the bed. My brother's sitting at his desk.

"Hey, Mack — how you doing?" he asks. "Good game?"

"Yeah," I say. I look at him and he smiles at me. Me and my brother, we don't say much to each other anymore.

"How'd it go at work today?" he asks.

I got to laugh. "Great, kid. Great." He tries, you got to admit that. "How'd it go at school?" I say. "Get much tail?"

"Ah, Mack," he says, turning away.

"Which you like best — white meat or dark meat?" He shrugs. "I take what I can get."

"Oh yeah — you a real lover, brother."

"I get mine," he says.

"Sure you do," I say. "Sure." I drink some beer. "Don't pay for it either."

"Sure," I say. He goes back to his work. I get up and sit down on the other end of the bed, next to him. I poke him in the arm and he looks at me. I stare him down. "Let me ask you something, Ronnie," I say. "What you gonna be when you grow up?"

"Ah, come on, Mack — leave me alone, huh?"

I rub my hand over his hair, he twists away. "What greasy hair you got, boy." I rub my hand over his head again.

"Cut it out, Mack," he says, twists away, angry now.

"Who's gonna make me?" I ask.

"Why you got to be like this?" he asks. He looks me straight in the eyes this time. I laugh in his face, then go for his head again. He pushes my hand away. "Come on," he says. "Cut it out. I got work to do."

"You a real good boy, Ronnie," I say to him. "Oh yeah. You gonna be a credit to your people some day — even if you do got kinky hair." I stand up, grab his head with both my hands, then hold it against my chest and rub my knuckles into his scalp. He shoves against me and twists away. He's fighting mad the way I like, backs up against the door, behind him I hear the old man shouting at the TV. I go for his head again, he tries to block my right hand, I sneak my left one under, get him around the waist good. The air goes out of him. He struggles but it don't help and soon I got him down on the bed, I'm tickling crap out of him. He rolls around, tries to keep my fingers away from his ribs. "You dirty mother — " he says. I grab him on the inside of his leg and squeeze. He don't scream because of my mother but his eyes, they on fire now. He's okay, I think. He's my brother. "You like shark bites?" I ask, squeeze harder. He got my wrists but he can't get me loose of him, I let go his leg and press my body against him, pin him to the bed. I reach down and pick up the can of beer. "How you like some beer, brother?"

"Come on — you'll get the bed wet!" he says.

"You do it every night anyway," I say. I try to grab his chin, keep it still, but when I do he gets away and knocks me on the floor. Some beer spills. He stands over me, taking breaths. "You're lucky I'm a merciful guy," he says. "Otherwise I'd kick shit out of you."

Then we both laugh. "Here," I say, standing up and offering him my beer.

"Nah," he says, goes back to his desk, tucks his shirt in. "I really got to work."

"Sure," I say. I lean back and relax, drink my beer. My brother studies and I don't bother him now. When the phone rings I figure it's the Penguin but it's this other guy from the newspapers. "My name is Ben Rosen," he says. "Maybe you have heard of me. I write sports for the *New York Star*."

"I heard of you," I say. I remember him, a half-pint guy with a big nose, always snooping around locker rooms at the Garden.

"Good. Well, I'll tell you why I am calling, Mack. I would like to meet with you. You see, I have this idea for a magazine article, what we call a profile — the story of you and what has happened to you in the five years since — since you left college." He stops. "So what do you think? If the article sells — who knows? — there might be something in it for you."

"How much?"

He laughs, sort of a cackle. "No evasions with you, heh?"

"How much?"

"It will be worth your while, Mack, I can promise you that. Please. Why don't we meet and talk first, all right?"

"How come you pick me?" I say.

"Ah," he says. "Why did I pick you, Mack? Because in you I see the perfect example of how big-time col-

lege sports ruthlessly exploits the young athletes of our
nation. How's that?" He laughs. "Because of your
race and your great talent, I see you as the symbol of
all those boys who have been victimized. And then
there is something else about you, Mack." His voice
drops down, like he's telling me a secret. "Of all the
boys, you were the only one who never said he was
sorry. I remember that."

"Mister," I say. "You got your story wrong. I was
sorry. You don't know how sorry I was when they
turned that money off."

"I like that, Mack," he says. "I like that. Yes. I
think we understand one another, if you know what I
mean —"

"Look," I say. "I got things to do. What you want?"

"What do I want? I want to help you, Mack. I
promise — it will be worth your while just to talk to
me."

"Where you want to meet?"

"What's convenient for you, Mack? Remember —
you are still the star."

"I'll be at the corner of Flatbush and Church at
nine," I say.

"I'll recognize you," he says, then laughs again. "As
they say, you will stand out in the crowd, heh?" I
hang up and go back into my room, drink some beer.
Soon my sister comes home and everybody crowds
around her, asking her how school was today and my
mother sets down a plate in front of her. I wait and
go into the kitchen after my old man and Ronnie come
back.

"Hi, Mack!" Selma says. She gets up, gives me a kiss on the cheek. She got to stretch way up to do it. Selma's real pretty. She got big brown eyes and a little nose and the lightest skin of any of us. When she was young she did some modeling a few times for some magazine. Now she goes to Brooklyn College. She be finished soon, then she go to work as a teacher. When I was at college in Ohio she come out to visit me once and I got her a date and we went to a dance and had a good time. We used to do lots of things together. "How are things going?" she asks.

"Okay," I say, sit down across from her, watch the way she tears a piece of bread at the corner of her mouth.

"You want a glass of milk?" my mother asks. I say no and she talks to Selma for a while with questions about school. She's real proud of Selma and Ronnie. They gonna be something, she says. Me, I'm the black sheep of the family, I guess. Oh yeah. Bet Rosen would like that, me a black sheep. Selma talks about this meeting she went to, my mother eats it up, keeps moving her head up and down. "The nice thing is," Selma says, "we had about forty percent Negroes there tonight. That's the most ever."

"That's good," my mother says. In back of the ballgame I hear Ronnie start to practice his bass. He starts with these exercises with the bow but after a while he puts on the radio and plucks with his fingers the way I like.

"You got to take me along to a meeting with you, sister," I say. "Help set me free — "

She's munching on a cookie, she smiles, the crumbs fall out of her mouth. "You mean it?" she says.

"Sure," I say. "Why not?"

"That's right," my mother says. "Maybe you introduce him to one of your nice friends." She grabs my ear and lifts me straight out of my seat. "We gotta get him married soon." She spins me around and points a big steak knife at me. "When you gonna get married, Mack?" She shoves me back against the dishes cabinet with the knife at my throat. "Come on, you. When you gonna get married? Answer quick!" She jabs the knife toward me and when I throw up my hand in front of my face she breaks out laughing. "Oh Mack!" she says, sits down again. "You see his face, Selma?" Selma laughs. I sit down. "Oh, you see his face? Who'd marry that face?" She reaches her hand over and rubs my cheek. "I'll tell you something I believe, though," she says. "There are lots of problems in this life — we've had our share, right?" Selma nods. "Right, Mack?" She raises her voice.

"Sure."

"So if you go to these meetings, and I'm not saying you shouldn't — but when you get together socially with people not of your race you got to watch yourself, that's all. Don't start nothing you can't finish."

"Oh mother!" Selma says, getting up.

"You sit down!" my mother says, grabs the knife. Selma sits. Don't none of us mess with my mother when she's got something to say. They go on for a while, building, both of them getting more upset, when they're yelling and screaming at each other I get up and walk out. Ever since Selma got mixed up in this meeting stuff we got fights galore. You ask me, though, it's my mother started something she don't want to finish. She the one moved us out of where we were into this neighborhood. Now Ronnie going to this Music and Art place and Selma being on committees and going to parties where everybody loves each other. I got to laugh. She the one give Ronnie the music lessons, she the one always teach us about how we're all equal. Man, I want to say, what you want? But I keep my mouth shut. I cause enough trouble.

I go in my room and get my sweater, Ronnie, he's bopping away, picking strings and talking to himself. He got the radio up loud so you can't hear the ballgame. "It's snatch-hunting time, brother," I whisper in his ear. "You want to come get some?"

He stops and turns down the radio. "Where you going?" he asks.

"I just told you."

"Nah. Where you going really?"

"Shit, man, I told you. I ain't had any for three days now." He looks away when I talk about this stuff. "Brother, when I was your age —"

"Oh, can it already, huh? I don't want to hear. I know all about what you were banging when you were my age."

"Mmm," I say, licking my lips. "I got the taste already."

"Ah, grow up, Mack."

"You got to get it up before you can grow up,"
I say. He looks away. "I'm going. You coming?"

He shakes his head.

"You got to be crazy to stay here," I say, "Crazy
people stay here."

All the starch wash out of his body. He sits down,
fiddles with a pencil. "See you, lover," I say, walk out,
poke my head in the kitchen. Selma's drying the dishes
and my mother's washing, they still talking, calm
now, with Selma trying to explain about things to
come. Only one thing coming, you ask me, that's
trouble. "I'm going out to get me a wife," I say.

"Oh you stink, Mack," Selma says. "Can't you be
serious? Ever?"

"I'm the most serious man that ever lived," I say.
"I need a wife to put some fun back in me."

"Mack's a good boy," my mother says. Selma sighs
and I move quick out the door. It's cool outside and
fat Julie got his back to me, sitting with his portable
radio up near his ear, blasting out the ballgame. Some
other folks sitting on the stoop, watching the cars.
Julie's father's next to him, reading a newspaper by
the light from over the door. His father likes me,
used to give me quarters when I was a kid to take
Julie for walks around the block. That was after Julie
had to be in a wheelchair. I remember, he was a kid,
he could walk. He got sick slow. Now when his head
goes all the way to one side somebody got to push
it up for him. He got no control of his muscles.

"Hello, Mack," Mr. Rubin says. "It's good to see

you —" Julie sees it's me now, he points on the tray in front of him and his father plugs something into the side of the radio, then puts the other end into Julie's ear so I don't hear. Mr. Rubin looks at me like I should try to understand. "See you, Mr. Rubin," I say, going down the steps. "Hang in there, Julie."

I get to Church Avenue I think about Rosen. What he want? All these guys always wanting to know why I did it, they give me a pain. I did it for money, what they think? The college paid me, I did what they wanted; gamblers paid, I worked for them; bookies paid more than gamblers, I sign up with them. Shit, man, nobody give me an education cause they like my looks. The college, they got their money's worth — they turn people away from their gates, I played there.

What I want to see Rosen for? I keep walking up Nostrand Avenue, to Linden Boulevard. Oh Mack, you got it made, man. Oh yeah, your mother move you straight into that white boy's schoolyard, you been flying high ever since. You grow up in that schoolyard, everybody tell you you can *be* something. You gonna be a great star someday, huh? You the only jig ballplayer down there when you eleven, twelve, everybody real nice to you. Oh yeah. Every week somebody sitting next to your ass, asking you things, older guys giving you hints, telling you how good you gonna be. The war ends, all these ballplayers coming back like heroes from killing dirty Japs and Nazis, guys crowd around them like they smiling Ike himself. Big Ed, he's the best. Everybody say he gonna

be great, the Army didn't mess him up. Fulks and
Mikan and Zaslofsky, they gonna have to make room
for Big Ed. I got to laugh, his size now, but I sitting
there then, lapping it up, figure this guy's some kind
of God. He comes back, though, I see how good he
is. He sits next to me between games, tells me I'm
gonna be good, how you gonna fight that? Me, I'm
floating over that backboard. Oh yeah. I got stories
for Rosen, how smart I was.

I got to do something. I'm down past the Linden
Theater and I look in this bar, keep walking. I'm not
paying for it tonight. I go into a drugstore, call up
this old girlfriend, but she says her husband's home.
I get out of the phone booth and look through the
magazines, James Dean, he gonna talk to you from
the dead. I see *The Amboy Dukes*, take a copy, put
it in my pocket. Maybe I can read it at work. In school
we used to look through the hot parts. The owner,
he looks at me, I know he seen me put the book in
my pocket, but he don't say nothing. Who's he scared
of? I go by, he looks at his shelves like he's trying to
figure something out. Outside I got the feeling somebody's tailing me. Since I left home I got that feeling.
I got nothing else to do, I wind up at the Penguin's
house on Martense Street. Inside the lobby I see somebody go up the stairs quick. From the shadow, it looks
like Big Ed. What's he doing here? I get in the elevator and go up, when I ring the Penguin's bell his
wife answers.

"Hello, Mrs. Penguin," I say and she laughs.

"Come on in," she says. "It's Mack — !" she calls.

The Penguin comes bouncing to us. He's got these bermuda shorts on, a T-shirt keeping his belly in. "Mack babe!" he says, grabs my hand and pumps it. "Boy it's good to see you! How've you been? Come on in, come on in! Bev — get Mack some food or something. What you want, Mack babe? Beer? A sandwich? I got the ballgame on. You want to watch?" He keeps jabbering, I got to laugh. We called him the Penguin because he looks just like the guy in Batman. His real name is Marty, but even his wife calls him the Penguin. He used to carry an umbrella with him around school to all our games when he was manager. He left it home once, I had my worst game, eight points.

"Here," I say, handing him *The Amboy Dukes*. "I got you a present."

He giggles, I go by, sit myself down in the living room and look at the TV. Soon he comes in carrying a bowl of fruit. I take an apple and he works on a banana. "I was just thinking about you, you know that?" he says. "They had this write-up in the papers tonight about the rookies with the pro basketball clubs and I was thinking how you could put them all in your hip-pocket. You could have been the greatest, Mack babe. Better than Stokes and Schayes and the Cooz. You know that?"

"And you could have been a ball boy for the pros, huh, Penguin?"

"C'mon, be serious, huh? Don't you think you could have been as good as these guys? I mean, you had everything, Mack! Remember how you went wild in the Garden in the championship in '49? Hell, all the coaches from the colleges who were scouting you, they said you were the greatest natural ballplayer to ever come out of New York! And remember the game you scored 33 against Boys High? Jeez, Mack, if. . . ." He keeps going the way he does, photographing my games back to me. After a while, he's out of high school, up to our first year in college. He still loves my ass for that. When the guys from the university come to me with the final papers, signing me up so I didn't go nowhere else with that letter of intent jazz, I just asked them where the scholarship for the Penguin was. I said I couldn't score without him and his umbrella, couldn't sign that letter till they give the Penguin his letter too. He's leaning over toward me, banana crud on his lips. "Remember when we got those two sorority chicks in Columbus?" he whispers.

"Yeah."

"We had some good times, huh, Mack? We did okay, you and me!"

"Hey look," I say, put my arm around his shoulder. "I got an idea." His eyes light up. "How bout if I bring my jock straps over here, you wash 'em —" I figure this to crush him, but he just giggles some more, tells me what a sense of humor I got. I look at him, I keep thinking he's twenty, thirty years older than me. "How's business?" I ask.

"Not bad," he says. The Penguin, he runs a men's clothing place on Flatbush Avenue with his father.

"How come you never come in? I told you I can get special clothes in that'll fit you just right — give it to you at cost, too. You know that, Mack."

"That's right," I say. "I got to get new clothes for where I work, my job."

"Ah, c'mon," he says. "Get some new clothes — make you feel good *in*side, Mack. You know what I mean? Don't be so down on yourself." He peels another banana. "When you come through the door tonight I said to myself, Mack's down on himself. Look at that long face." He shrugs. "But what can I do for you, Mack? I mean, I'm glad you stopped by, but a young guy like you shouldn't be spending his time with married folks, he should be out living it up. If I had what you had, I'd be knocking off stuff all over Brooklyn every night of the week. How come, Mack? How come you're so down on yourself? Look, I'll admit your job's not the greatest in the world, but it's not permanent. You got two years of college — why can't you do something better?"

"Oh yeah," I say. "I gonna make something of myself, huh?"

He blinks his eyes up and down, then takes my hand in his. "Hey, I didn't say nothing wrong, did I? I didn't mean anything, Mack. Jeez — I wouldn't try to tell you how to run your life. It's just that I think you ought to cheer yourself up." He giggles. "Maybe if you had a wife, we could swap or something, like they say these young executives do." It's the ninth inning and the Giants are down by three. "How do you like that Sal the Barber? Can't he shave 'em, though? Only guy who hits him solid is Mays. He got a spell or something over the others." He scratches the hair on his chest like a monkey. "Hey Bev!" he calls. "What the hell are you doing in the kitchen so long?" She yells back that she's making coffee. "She talks about you sometimes," the Penguin says. "She thinks you're sweet — ain't that something? Boy, if she knew about the things we did together! Remember, after we won the divisional title by beating Madison in '48, when we all went to the Fox together and picked up those girls in the balcony? You were a killer, Mack! Remember how you kept saying you were Alan Ladd's twin brother?"

I get up. "I want a drink of water," I say.

"Let Bev bring it."

"I'll get it," I say, duck my head to get through to the kitchen.

"Coffee'll be ready in a minute," she says.

"I just want some water."

She gets up from reading the paper. "I'll get it," she says. She goes to the sink and I watch her twitch her butt. She's small like the Penguin, but built okay. Tight ass. She got slacks and a red sweater on, I got a feeling she knows I like what I see. She got the glass under the faucet when I put my hand on her ass. Her head comes up to my chest. She shuts the water off, turns around like she expected it, stands with her back to the sink. I drink and put the glass down on the drain-rack, then press in on her, she smiles. I step back, she brushes her hair once with her hand and sits down at the table. She smiles at me. "C'mere," she says. "Screw you," I say, walk back into the living room. I look at the Penguin, sitting back in his chair, his feet just about reach the floor.

"I was just thinking," he says. "Remember that motel we stayed at when we were in the tournament in San Francisco, and that chink chambermaid? Boy —" I listen to him go on about what was. Him and Rosen, they the ones should get together. His wife brings in coffee and cake and we shoot the shit some more, then I leave. I walk back to Nostrand Avenue but I don't feel like going home yet. What I gonna do there? Some people coming out of the subway at Church Avenue. The trolleys used to be there, we'd hitch rides on the backs. There was this comic book had the life story of Pete Gray, the one-armed ballplayer who played for the Browns during the war. Man, I loved him! When he'd catch the ball he'd toss it up, grab his glove off under his armpit with his stump, catch that ball with his good hand before it come down. Then he'd throw. He lost his arm when he was a kid hitching rides on backs of trucks and things. After I read the story I didn't ride the trolley cars no more.

I still got the feeling somebody's after my ass. I look back quick, some guy ducks into a hallway. I get who it is, he be one bloody heap. I get on the bus, figure I'll get off, walk around the old neighborhood. Sometimes I do that. I don't stick out so much down there, people don't know who I was. When I get home it's late, my old man's still sitting up, watching some movie on TV. I go into my room, sit on my bed and when I take my shoes off and throw them down, Ronnie turns over. I put the light on so I can see what I'm doing. He sits up and rubs his eyes.

"Hi, Mack," he says. "You have a good time tonight?"

"Sure." He covers his eyes from the light with his hand. "Go to sleep," I say. "Sorry I had to turn the light on —"

"That's okay," he says and grabs the covers, ducks his head under. I hang my clothes up and wash, feel like talking to him, but by the time I go over, smooth my hand over his head, he don't move, so I just go to sleep.

TWO

I COME HOME from work, Julie's real sick my mother says, she's down in his apartment all the time, helping Mrs. Rubin with him. "Why don't you go downstairs and say hello to him," she says. "He'd like that."

"Sure," I say. "He ain't said a word to me for five years —"

"Well, you got to be tolerant of sick people, Mack." She lets out a long sigh. "It'll take a miracle to save that poor boy. But maybe it's for the best. Maybe the Lord has figured it's time to relieve him and his poor family from their burdens." So I go downstairs after supper with Ronnie. First we go out to the candy store, get him a few sports magazines. In front of the house some kids are playing boxball. They all say hello to Ronnie, he roughs them on the hair, they love it. He's getting pretty big. I guess he's the hero now. He's got something on his mind too, I know, but he don't say nothing yet. We ring the bell, Mrs. Rubin comes to the door, says how glad she is we came. We go into Julie's room, he's sitting in his wheel chair, watching a war movie on TV.

"We brought you some stuff," Ronnie says and lays it all out in front of him. His head is all the way to one side and his father straightens it out. He don't look so good. It's the first time in about eight years

I'm in his room and it still looks the same. The walls are covered with color pictures, Pee Wee and Willie Mays and Cousy and a picture of the '47 Dodgers with all these guys I forgot about like Bruce Edwards and Vic Lombardi and Spider Jorgenson. His room is real big, full of all kinds of junk, records and magazines and newspapers and comic books. Next to his bed there's a picture in a gold frame of him with Dean Martin and Jerry Lewis. I remember when I saw him on TV with them, asking for money. I used to come down at nights sometimes and stay with him when his folks had to go out. Before they had TV we used to make up scorecards with a ruler and pencil like you get at the ballpark and keep track of what was going on from the radio. He had this erector set with a motor and we made a big windmill once, and this make-believe radio kit, where you had a microphone and things to make sound effects with. We used to make up these shows on our own, me, I played Ivan Shark and he was Captain Midnight. I had some crazy laugh, just like the guy on the radio. He could use his hands then, work those steel brushes to make the sound of trains, and the coconut shells for horses when we did the Lone Ranger or Straight Arrow. A lot of times we'd just sit around and read comic books — Batman and the Blackhawks and Captain Marvel. My favorite was Plastic Man. I used to walk through the streets — flash! — change myself into telephone booths and lampposts, parade around the room, my arms and legs gangling in all directions, Julie'd go hysterical. I'd stand outside the room, reach

my arm around the corner without coming in, take
something off a shelf. In the classic comics I liked
the Corsican Brothers best. They were born attached
and when one of them felt pain, even if they were in
different countries, the other guy felt it too.

Man, I say to myself, you just like the rest, living
in what was. You better cut that crap, Mack! I look
at Julie and he's got pajamas on, his head's pushed
forward and the bottom of his face is like a mongolian
idiot. There's spit drooling out of the side of his
mouth, it takes all his strength to push one of the
magazines away so he can see the ones under it. His
father talks to him, saying isn't it nice we come down
and I figure, Julie's got a brain left he knows the
score, what's the only thing could bring me into his
room. I'm sorry I listened to my mother, but what
can I do now? I was Plastic Man, I could spread
out into some molding on the wall, squeeze down
into a TV tube.

"How you been, Julie?" I ask, his head drops to his
shoulder, his father straightens it again. His mother's
in the doorway, biting on her lip so she don't cry, she
asks us if we want some milk and cookies and I say
we can only stay a minute or two. Ronnie talks for
a while, he's pretty good at seeming natural about it.
He asks Julie if he thinks getting Dale Mitchell will
sew up the pennant for the Dodgers. Julie keeps his
eyes on his tray. I remember when this organization
for guys like him used to come around during the
summer and take him to a ballgame, I used to go

along, get five bucks a day for wheeling him. He came
to see me play in the Garden when I was a sophomore,
I stopped by before the game, got some of the other
studs on the team to come over, say hello to him. He
sat behind our bench, kept banging his program
against the side of his chair, moving his ass like he had
to leak. "As long as you're here, maybe you could do
me a favor, boys," Mr. Rubin says, "and help me get
Julie into bed."

"Sure," Ronnie says. I shrug and Julie goes mad in
his seat, like he's crapping, moaning and things. I go
around the front and start to slide the tray out from
its runners the way I remember and his face goes
wild red and he lets out this sound from his throat
like he's an ape. He slides his arm along the tray and
knocks a magazine we bought him off. It takes all his
strength. "Maybe you better do it yourselves," I say.
I shove my hands out, show everybody my palms.
"He don't want my stinking hands to touch him!"

Then they all say these things to try to make me feel
better but I don't give a shit. My old lady's right,
he'd save everbody a burden. Mr. Rubin says they
better do it the usual way and he pushes the chair
over to the bed and I watch. Last time they paid me
to help you could still lift him. He must weigh over
two-fifty now. They got this big contraption at the
foot of his bed that swings over like a derrick with
this long silver arm out over it, got straps hanging.
Ronnie tries to help but Mrs. Rubin motions him back.
We both watch. "Hey, you build that with your

erector set, Julie?" I ask. Mr. Rubin's gasping for breath, sliding this seat thing under Julie's ass like he's in the parachute jump at Coney Island. Mrs. Rubin turns a few knobs and the crane swings out. Then Mr. Rubin puts this straightjacket thing behind Julie's neck to keep it braced, grabs him by the feet. Mrs. Rubin turns a handle and a minute later fat Julie's floating up off his chair and Mr. Rubin's guiding him toward the bed, gets him level, shoves his body on. "Maybe for Christmas we'll get that electric motor the organization recommended," Mrs. Rubin says. "Won't that be nice? So much more comfortable."

Upstairs, my mother says some guy been calling but wouldn't leave a name. Selma comes home and nobody can come near her, she got to finish a term paper. Bilko's on TV and my old man is laughing his head off. "That's the way it was," he keeps saying. My old man, he's a big hero. Got his hand blown off when a stove exploded in a kitchen in Fort Belvoir. My mother says we all got to be nice to him, the doctor says the explosion did something to him, if he gets put away somewhere we don't get as much money from the government. I remember when he had a bandage over the stump, fat and white. "Aw, Sarge," Doberman says and my old man roars. "Ain't he something!" I go back into the bedroom.

"Who's this guy who keeps calling?" Ronnie asks, but he got something else on his mind. I don't answer. "I guess it's none of my business," he says, then looks at me with his soul in his eyes. He tries again. "Remember that basketball uniform you gave me?" he asks.

I look at him. It's the first time he's talked about basketball since I can remember. "I didn't give it to you. The school paid."

He laughs, forces it. "What's the difference? How old was I then?"

He's after something, I go along. "That was my senior year," I say. I figure: two years of college plus five since makes it seven or eight, makes him eight, maybe seven then. "Why you ask?"

"Just wondering," he says. "I was thinking about it today at school." He shrugs and shifts in his chair. "I don't know if I really remember being the mascot of the team or not — or whether I've just thought about it so much and people used to tell me about what I looked like that I talked myself into believing I actually remember. You know what I mean? You ever have that feeling — that your memory of something has been replaced by your memory of the memory?" He laughs, shrugs his shoulders the way he does. "I don't make much sense, do I? At school some kids think I'm a real goofball the way I go on talking about things like this. We had this big discussion in English about whether things are real or not, you know? We saw this movie by Mark Twain about a guy with a million bucks who gets everything he wants because nobody got change for it. But he never uses any money — so is the note real or not? Gregory Peck plays the guy — you see it?"

"No."

"Anyway, I think I remember one thing when I was a mascot, to get back to what I started talking about — I'm always getting side-tracked. That's what happens in school. I start talking about one thing and I wind up on the other side of China." He laughs some more, pretty free. "I'm doing it again now, huh? It's nutty. Anyway, I got this vague memory of you holding me up in the air and me dropping the ball through the hoop. I was sure fat then! Boy, I wish I was now, you know?" He stretches out his arm toward me. "Look how goddamned skinny I am. Guess what I weigh?"

"One-seventy, seventy-five —"

"Just about one-sixty — and I'm over six feet! Six-one and a half. You think I oughta lift weights?"

"Do what you want, kid."

"Am I bugging you?" he asks. "I don't want to be a pest or anything, so you shut me up if you got things to do."

"Oh yeah, I got lots of things to do. Got to check with my stockbroker."

"Is that the guy who's been calling?"

"Sure," I say.

"Do you know anything about weights? They say that it builds you up, but that if you stop lifting the muscle turns right into flab —" He goes on like this till I move out, get some beer. I pass Selma in the living room, she hardly knows I'm alive. She got a pencil in her mouth, she's muttering she'll never finish on time. My mother's sitting next to my father, her tired legs up, he's guzzling down whiskey, the TV staring at them. I go back to my room, Ronnie's still waiting. "Okay," I say. "Lay it down, babe. What you got on your mind? You've been leading to something all night —"

"I suppose so," he says, lets out air. "Thanks — I needed you to push it out of me, Mack. Okay. It's like this, see. They're having tryouts for the varsity basketball team in two weeks and I was thinking of going out for it — in gym, the coach came over to me and asked me how come I didn't go out last year. He says I'd have a good chance, so I was thinking maybe you could help me. That's what all that jazz was about when I was a mascot and stuff." He says it all pretty quick. "Will you help me?"

"Sure," I say.

He jumps up. "You mean it? Jesus, Mack, that'd be great! I'm not like you were, but for my school I'm pretty good. I mean, we got a lot of real fruity guys and nobody much bigger than me, either, and I'd kind of like to be on a team once, you know? If you'd give me a few pointers — you know, tell me what I'm doing wrong and things, man, I'd be in like Flynn!"

"Yeah," I say.

He's so excited, my "yeah" makes him put brakes on. "Look, if you don't want to — he says.

"I'll do it," I say. "Didn't I say so?"

He don't press me, seeing me mad. He shifts around, makes believe he's doing homework. "Anytime you got free time, let me know," he says, his back to me. "No rush, I mean."

"Sure," I say. Then I get up to move out again, get this big black turtleneck sweater out of my bottom drawer and put it on, take a pair of shades out of the top drawer and slip them in my pocket, no sense having everybody ask why I'm wearing them at night. In the Village, those shades and the sweater, that's the stuff, man. Oh yeah. With them and my skin I don't need to but mumble a few words to get the meat I need. I get on the IRT at Church and Nostrand, remember how those cheerleaders would squeal and groan before games, smile at me, jump up and split their legs, throw themselves back so their tits bounced up and down in their sweaters. Oh yeah, I had a golden dick, those days.

I'm sitting at this table in the back, got a broad by my side asking my opinions on things, if I'm the black brother she wants to love, I say fine. Then this wait-ress comes by the first time, her butt twitching from side to side between the chairs, like Hugh McElhenny jitterbugging down a football field, her tray with drinks and sandwiches held out over everybody's head, she bends down quick and whispers in my ear: "Who you trying to fool with that get-up, black boy?" Then she's gone. "That's Willa!" somebody says. I don't see her face the first time. I got my arm around this blond-haired bitch, rubbing her cheek, she comes by again. I see her face this time and it's broad and flat and pock-filled. Ugly as hell, like Selma might have looked if she was bigger and had a truck mash her in. She got one tooth outlined with gold and it catches the light. "Hey you," she says. "What's wrong with your own kind?" I let my arm come back to my side, kids all around me, they laugh. Willa winks, swivels off.

"Isn't she something?" my broad says to me.

"Do you know her?" someone else asks.

"Sure," I say. "Yeah. We went to college together." They go for this, I give them more, tell them we were in plays together, give them a load about how we were in summer stock and things, from their eyes, they wishing on what we had in the sack together. Willa comes by a couple times, just winks. I keep my hands off the chicks where she can see, but under the table I do my work, she likes it. Where I gonna take her? Nowhere I bet, but I don't give a shit, at least the time is going by. I drink and watch them pass a joint around in front of me, you don't get me to blow on it. Through the smoke they got Willa at the table now, repeating to her the things I said. She laughs this big horse laugh, pounds this skinny guy on the back. "Didn't I tell you that? So what? Waiting on tables beats it all. Right?" Must be good for tips, I figure. "What else Mack here been telling you?" she asks.

How she know my name? She's around in back of me, I'm feeling funny. She takes my shades off, bends down and presses her cheek next my forehead. "Me and Mack were the lovers of lovers!" she says, laughing. Then she twists my ear real hard so it hurts. "Ain't that so, Mack honey? — You kids don't make him do nothing bad now, hear? We wouldn't want to get Mack into no fix!" she says, then howls and takes off. Screw her, I say, and drink some more. They got a group of kids up front now playing on guitars and banjos, I can't stand it, get up. By the door some guy got his eye on me, I can't make him out. I get up, he moves out. Me, too. There's sweat all inside my sweater and shirt. This bitch grabs my hand, I shove her down. Oh yeah, I'm tough, me. "I'll be back," I say. "You play jacks a while, babe." Then I'm gone through the door and the cold air, that's better. I keep my shades off to see where that guy is, I start walking, I'm at the subway across from the Waverly Theater, I hear the voice behind me.

"Hey, Mack, wait up, babe!"

It's Willa, she got her coat half on over her uniform. "What you want?" I say.

She sticks her arm into mine, guides me up Sixth Avenue. "How you feel?" she asks. We're sliding along the fence to the schoolyard and she points into it. "How's your jump shot? I'll play you one-on-one, you spot me three baskets, ten baskets wins, huh?" She yanks me by the arm and we stop, her staring straight into my eyes with her gold-edged tooth. "Do you still snort?" she asks, then throws her head back and howls. "You had the moves, Mack — and you snorted like a wild-eyed hog, driving toward that basket. Fire out of your nose, babe!" She yanks again, away from the schoolyard. "Let's go, let's go, huh?"

"What's your game, babe?" I say.

"Willa's my name, waiting's my game —" She laughs. I look at her, down, see that she comes about to my shoulder, two inches less than Ronnie maybe, she's big. "Are you married yet? Tell me that, Mack. You married?"

"No," I say. What she want? She hustles us across the street and we're past the other entrance to the subway, in front of the bank. They got a sign in the window telling you to vote.

"Too bad — everybody should be married. I was married. Still am, if you want to get technical." She jabs my ribs. "You want to get technical?"

"How you know me?" I ask. "How bout answering that?"

"You don't remember me, huh?" she says. I look around. People huddling around the green newsstand buying papers. Down the street behind me I think I see the guy been following me. When I stop he does. I start back a step and the guy disappears. "Are you? Hey, man, wake up!" she says, tugging my sweater. "Are you?"

"Am I what?"

"Coming home with me?"

"Sure. Why not?"

"I like your enthusiasm," she says and we're moving right on Eighth street past all the stores. "You'll see my kid, but he'll be sleeping. Mrs. Fontanez downstairs watches him when I'm at work. How many kids you got?" My head's about as good as it's gonna be the rest of this night so I stop, push her against a window, got brassieres and panties and stuff in it. "Look," I say. "What's the scoop? Talk and talk fast. Where you know me from and how you know about me and what you want?"

She twists her wrist loose quick and shoves her ugly puss right up against my face. "Oh man, how you get to be so tough?" she says. "You got me *so* scared. You a real man, Mack, huh? Oh, you a real man!"

"C'mon," I say, and raise my hand.

"You gonna hit me? Oh my!" She laughs, lets her head rest a second on my chest, then lifts away quick. "If your eyes weren't so bleary we'd tease you a while longer, but it ain't that much fun, you being so serious. Where's the fun in you?" She turns her head right and left. "Hey — why we walking down this street? I don't live here. I live uptown, the other way. Rents down here are sky-high. You live around here?"

"No."

"Where you live?"

"What's the difference?"

She lets out this laugh again, like she's half swallowing it. "Come on, Mack love, where you live?"

"Okay. I live at home."

I expect her to laugh, but she don't. "This way," she says, and we're moving back toward the avenue again. "You can call from my place, tell you're not coming home."

"I don't got to call."

"You got a mother?"

"Yeah."

"Well, she'll worry so you'll call. How you feeling now? Your head clear?"

"I'm doing all right."

"Where's all your tongue?" she says. "You leave

it back at *Mario's?* You had plenty of tongue for those
nice little Eva's and now all you can do is dribble out
a couple of words to me. Why you think that is?"
Then she swings from one side of me to the other.
"I had a feeling I'd meet somebody, you know? Mrs.
Fontanez, she got charts and books and mystic balls
and there's been a tall dark stranger in my future ever
since before little Willie was born. Hey — you wanna
know why I call him Willie? Cause when he comes
and there's just me and him I figure we're in the same
boat and it's only fair we call each other by the same
thing. So when I'm alone and look at him and talk to
him I can talk to me, too. That sound loony to you?"
She shrugs. "Who cares if it does — but does it?"
I don't say nothing. "Oh man," she says. "Why you so
close to the vest with me, huh? Loosen up, Mack.
Loosen up those long limbs of yours." She stops, pulls
the bottom of my right eyelid down. "You don't look
so good," she says. The next thing, we're in a cab
together, going through Central Park and over to the
West Side, she talks the whole time, which is okay
with me. What I got to say? "You like Central Park?"
she asks. "I take Willie there in the mornings, mornings being afternoons, but I call them mornings because they're when we wake up. Do you?"

"Do I what?"

She drops her head on my shoulder, shakes it back
and forth. "You're too much, too much, Mack baby."
Everytime she says my name it bugs me and I ask her
again where she know me from but she don't say.

When we get out of the cab, we go down a few steps to a door behind a bunch of garbage cans, swing a black gate open. "Mrs. Fontanez and her husband are the super for this house and a few others on this block." She knocks on the door, Mrs. Fontanez comes, fat with hairs growing out of these browns marks on her face. I step back into the shadows. "You are home so early?" Mrs. Fontanez says. "How's he been?" Willa asks. "An angel," Mrs. Fontanez says. "A devil," Willa says. "No, an angel," Mrs. Fontanez says, and laughs. "This is a friend of mine, Mack Davis," Willa says and grabs me by the hand. "I am very pleased to be meeting you," Mrs. Fontanez says, one hand out to me, the other pulling her shirt closed over her tits. There's hairs there too. "Yeah," I say and Willa glares at me. "I'm pleased to meet you too," I say. "Willa's told me how good you are to Willie." Willa's eyes, they gleam at me, I figure I said the right thing. "Come inside for a minute," Mrs. Fontanez says. "I will clear away some —" "No, we couldn't," Willa says. "Some other time. We don't want to keep you up —" Mrs. Fontanez goes back inside.

"I knew the Mack I knew was there somewhere under that faggy disguise you got on," Willa says. "Times must be bad, though, you having to scrounge around for tail the way you do. Times are getting hard, boys. Mack's in town!" She laughs, then Mrs. Fontanez is back, Willa puts her arms out. "And here's little Willie. Come to mama, Willie baby. There now. Oh you ugly little thing. You the ugliest thing on this block!" She takes the baby in her arms and its eyes open. It's big and fat. "You figure him for a backcourt man or a pivot man?" Willa asks. "Or is he gonna be able to do everything the way you could?" She turns to Mrs. Fontanez. "Mack here could do it all!" "That is very nice," Mrs. Fontanez says, Willa kisses her and they hug each other up with the baby between, then we're up the stairs and up past the other stairs to the entrance and then we got three more sets to go and we're inside. Willa sets the baby down in the crib. It's brand new, looks like, with pictures of Snow White and her seven studs all around it. Her place is nice. I tell her.

"You surprised?" she asks, bending over little Willie and fixing a blanket on him. "All I got is this one room but it's enough for me and Willie — and a guest when we have one. You can use the couch there." "I wasn't planning on it," I say. She laughs again. "What were you planning on, Mack babe?" She leaves Willie, takes her coat off and comes to me. I'm sitting in this nice old rocking chair she got, facing this fireplace with a mirror and she runs her hands up my neck and fiddles with my ear. She leans over and kisses me on the forehead. "How about milk? You want some milk?" I go to grab her but she's gone toward the kitchen, in the corner of the room. "I got the moves too, huh?" she says, winking. There's a thing hanging from the ceiling with colored plastic and silver stuff that reaches into Willie's crib and it's spinning around now. "You make your phone call, I'll get the milk."

I call home, Ronnie answers, I tell him to leave a note on the kitchen table that I'll be home for supper tomorrow so nobody worries.

"Sure, Mack. Hey — I didn't say anything before that got you mad, did I?"

"No."

"You sure?"

"I said so, didn't I?"

"Okay — have a good time, Mack."

"Yeah."

I hang up and Willa smiles. "Okay," she says. "You did what I asked so I'll tell you what you want to know. You ready?" She gives me my milk and I sit down again, not feeling as restful as I did, but okay. "Oh Willa," she says. "Maybe you shouldn't tell him. This way you got mystery on your side, big Mack not knowing how you know all about him. You rather have me mysterious or you rather have me out in the open —?" She slaps me on the shoulder. "There's a lot in the open, about 170–175 pounds of pure Willa. So what you want?" I don't answer and she sighs, her mouth closes over her grinning teeth, more serious. "Okay. I was gonna tell you anyway. Why not?" Then she starts in about how she remembers me from when I played at Erasmus and she was a cheerleader for Commerce. We played them in the Garden in '47 and '48 and she says I spoke to her once. "Yeah — you told me to get off the court. You had a game that day! Automobile springs in your calves, Mack! We had leapers in our school too, but none like you." She tells me how she followed me in the papers when

I went to college, saved her money and got the best seats when I played in the Garden. "I practiced, too," she says. "My one hope, see, was that you'd make the '52 Olympics team — a cinch — and I'd make the woman's team and then you'd look at me. I was batty!" She shakes her head. "Then when the fixes hit I was shattered, you know? Yeah, guess you do, huh? —You know what else? When that Kellogg first told how he was bribed, I wanted to come see you real bad. I figured for sure you'd be involved. Why not?" She laughs, don't look at me. "When they caught you I even tried to blame myself some, saying if I hadn't been so shy maybe I could have helped you. Oh man, I was wired for trouble those years!" She stops. "I talk too much, huh?" I don't say anything. I'm tired and she knows it. It's quiet. "Willie's doing what we should do," she says. "What you thinking so much?"

"Nothing," I say and with the stuff in my head and her here bringing up those years again, I'm wondering. Maybe her and Rosen are in cahoots, her working for him. How come Ronnie pick tonight to ask me to coach him is what I want to know. I hear Willa saying things to me about times in high school she almost called me, things she did, but it comes from far now. I figure the guy following me got to wait outside all night now, hiding in doorways. Me, I'm Plastic Man, and I stretch my arms, slide them under the door and down the steps and out in the street until they get him and drag him all the way up. And fat Julie — who he think he is, not letting me touch him? It's real

warm inside my sweater, the drinks with the milk,
I get to remember this N.Y.U. sweatshirt Big Ed
gave me at the schoolyard. Where is it? I wore it
everywhere. Big Ed must weigh more than Julie by
now. They say he got a heart condition he gained so
much weight. After the fixes and jail they say he
didn't do nothing but stay home and eat. I tried to
see him once and called him, but the only time we
met was in the D. A.'s office. "You better get yourself
that broom now, Mack," Big Ed said to me. And "I'm
sorry. I'm sorry, Mack." That was all. I told him to
shove it, what was he sorry for, he didn't make me do
anything I didn't want to, but that broom, that's the
broom he told me about once in the schoolyard waiting for nexts.

"You know what Big Ed said?" I ask Willa. "He
said I had the stuff to make it." I remember, hear his
voice real close. 'Mack,' he says, his arm around my
shoulder. 'You can make it. You listen to me — if you
don't want to be a dumb jig janitor pushing a broom
around your whole life, you come down here and live
in this schoolyard the next few years. If you do that,
people gonna be kissing your ass and giving you
money and presents. You know why? Just because
you can put that ball through the hoop. You got real
market value, Mack, and you take advantage of it.
Market value, Mack! What anybody wants to give,
you take, hear? Because the minute something happens and you can't put that ball through the cords better than the next guy, they'll be sucking his ass and
you'll be left with nothing but a broom. So you take

what you can get while you get.' "We were good friends, me and Big Ed."

"I believe it," Willa says. "Now start getting your clothes off and get some sleep."

"Big Ed, he was a star at N.Y.U. before the war but when he come back something changed and he was good in the schoolyard, but that was it. Man, he dressed flashy. He was swift —"

"You're swift, too, Mack — swift out of them clothes."

"Did you know Big Ed?"

"No."

"Big Ed, he's the one got me into the fixes — but he wasn't the big guy — they never get the big guys. Poor Ed. Why it have to happen?"

"You just relax now, Mack. You just relax, babes —"

"Big Ed, he wasn't just good, he was smart, see? He could thread a needle with a pass. If him and me'd been on a pro team together, we'd have had it all. He knew the score. I didn't have to play bad to dump, see? 'You can score your load,' he said, 'but make your teammates look bad. You see a pass coming, you break the other way, then lunge back for it, see? If the game's close, you play your man close, foul him and then argue with the ref that you didn't. You get your coach and the fans on your side — but still, when you don't drive no more with four fouls on you, everybody knows why and nobody holds it against you. You got it? They take it out on the ref. There's ways, Mack. There's ways.'" I'm standing up near the crib, talking just like Big Ed used to, like I'm him, my arm around Willa like she's me, and I want her to understand how nobody was trying to hurt nobody. "Don't let 'em use you, Mack," I say. "You use them. Do you get me? Do you understand that? What are you getting from them? Minor league training with low pay and long hours. Don't be a sucker. Don't let 'em use you, Mack. You use them." Willa's saying something now, I hear Willie cry, I'm me and Big Ed's outside again, talking.

Next thing I know, Willa's on top of me banging on my chest, her thighs straddling my hips, she's got me pinned to the mat. "Hey!" I say, try to shove her off but she pins my wrists down. My head don't clear too quick and her jabbering and Willie's crying about break my skull. "It's seven-thirty," she says. "What time you got to be at work? Come on — what time?"

"Nine," I say, lying. Should be eight-thirty.

"Well, get your eyes working and move, man. We don't allow welfare cases here." Her eyes laugh and my breath stinks I can tell. Head's wooly too. I look across the room and see the couch is the way it was so I figure me and Willa shared the bed I'm in but I don't remember how. She lifts me by the ears, then slams my head down. "You're about as pretty as me in the morning," she says. "My, what big ears you got!" She got on this flannel gown and when she laughs her tits shake inside. I feel her weight on me. Strong meat. I go to grab her around the waist to get her flush on me, but I'm too slow. She bangs me once on the chest, and as she hops off gets me good in the stomach, low. "No time for fumbling, babe. You got to work. Get washed and Willie and I'll have breakfast for you. Ain't that right, Willie?" She's wrapping a big red plaid man's robe round her, snatching little Willie up out of his crib. He stops crying the minute she goes to him, makes these gurgling sounds. "Bathroom's out in the hall. To the left." She throws a towel at me and I sit up. All I got on are shorts. I wash and dress, she fixes breakfast, busy with little Willie most of the time, which is okay. "Off you go, big boy," she says when I'm done eating. "You know where we are?"

"What you mean?"

"The street, the street — where I live. What you think I mean?" I shrug. "Where you work? — Brooklyn?"

"Yeah."

She eyes me, Willie across her shoulder, sucking on his brown thumb. "You wanna tell me what you do?"

I laugh. "I work at the Minit–Wash," I say, "washing down cars, you know? That's how come I got such clean hands." That's funny so I laugh some more. "Yeah, me, I got the cleanest hands of any fixer around —"

She don't laugh with me. "You're okay," she says. "What subway you need? IRT is two and a half blocks to the left, at Broadway, IND to the right a few blocks down, by the Planetarium. That's quickest."

"How come you don't say nothing on where I work?" I ask.

"Beat it," she says.

"Hey, you gonna get into trouble for breezing out last night the way you did?"

"They don't like it, they know what they can do."

"Oh man, you're as tough as me, huh? You a real tough babe."

"Sure," she says, opens the door. "Say goodby to uncle Mack, Willie," she says, opening and closing her hand. Willie looks at me, heads back for her shoulder and his thumb. "Say bye–bye," she says. "Bye–bye." Willie don't move, can't con him. "He wants to be fed," she whispers to me. "Say bye–bye, Willie babe, my love, my ugly love. Uncle Mack's going. Say bye–bye." She jerks him around, hard, lifts his hand, and between the two of them they get his fingers wiggling at me, but he don't move his lips. I'm out the door and she starts to close it behind me.

"Hey, wait," I say.

"What for?"

"What happens next?"

She laughs. "Get to work."

"I mean, I gonna see you again?"

"You know where I live, you know where I work. Bye–bye, Mack." Then she howls her crazy laugh and slams the door. I hop down the stairs and get outside. The morning's gray like me, overhung and a yellow garbage truck is coming up the street. Some spic chicks walk by, black hair shining, tight skirts. I hear somebody calling me. I look both ways, then up. Willa's hanging out the window, holding Willie under one arm. "Watch out for deep waters, babe," she calls.

"You watch out now." Then the window cracks shut. I see Mrs. Fontanez half up the steps with a garbage can, so I run down the street left before she gets a chance to see me.

THREE

I GOT Rosen on my back and Willa on my mind. One makes up for the other, though. With me and Willa, it's good, what more I got to say to you? But Rosen, he's after my ass. He comes down to the carwash the first time, short and fat, shaped like an eggplant the way the Penguin is, I tell him I'm real sorry I forgot to meet him. "Tell me something," he says. "I'll bet you were surprised when I called — I'll bet you thought everybody had forgotten you."

"Me, I got a big fan club, Rosen," I say, then I tell him he's blocking business with his heap, does he want it washed. He says of course, I get in, move it into the booth, turn the water on and me and the guys do a job on it. His car's a mess, there's a bad stink coming from the back seat where he got dirty laundry thrown around. Smokey asks if he should hose him down, he must need a bath so bad, but I say I got a better idea. The car comes out the front end and Rosen starts gassing about his article, I look in his back window, ask him if he's going to the laundry. "I'd like to help a guy like you," I say, watch his eyes blink. "I mean you taking such an interest in me and all —" I grab a hose and spin the nozzle, let it spray into his back seat, nice and thin, the guys, they all laugh, I tell Rosen there's no extra charge, to come back soon.

The next day he's there. I figure he likes being

dumped on, so I dump, make him pay to get his car washed again, the guys and me, we got to laugh. He got this strange look in his eye — wild, man — but I don't let on it bugs me. Inside, his car's clean, no clothes and his papers all neat in this new leather job. "Sometimes people need a push, Mack," he says, seeing me look it over. "So you pushed and I did something." He stops, then puts his arm on mine like somebody died. "Maybe you need a push, Mack. You can do better than this. I know it."

"Sure," I say. "I can *be* something, right? Like a pro ballplayer maybe. Me and Sherm White — we gonna make the All-Star team this year."

He eyes me. "Ah," he says. "So! It does bother you! It—"

"Get off my back, Rosen," I say, mad, shoving him. "Okay? Just get off, man!"

"Mack, Mack! Be calm. I didn't intend any offense," he says, comes back for more. "I'm with you, don't you know that? Just give me a chance. That's all I ask. When you are through today, come over to my place and we'll talk. What do you have to lose?"

The next day this is what he writes in his column:

DOES ANYBODY REMEMBER?

By Ben Rosen

When the late Dr. James A. Naismith first fastened two peach baskets to the balcony of the International YMCA Training School at Springfield, Mass., he undoubtedly never envisioned the mass popularity that his evening recreational innovation would achieve.

There's no need to itemize the statistics that are evidence of the fact that basketball is the largest spectator sport in America — and, to judge from my own perennial tour of this city's gyms and school-yards — the one most participated in by this nation's youngsters.

Yes, basketball would seem to have come a long way since that wintery day in 1891 — but exactly how far has it really come? Dr. Naismith probably never envisioned the success of his game, but there's something else I'll wager he never envisioned. And that's the melancholy sight that greeted me yesterday when I stopped at a local car-wash. There, to my surprise, I met a boy to whom I used to devote many columns — a boy who should right now be earning the fame and fortune his talents deserve; a Negro boy from the streets of our city who is probably still one of the most adept hoopsters in the land. And what was he doing? He was washing down cars. Why? Because he was in the fixes.

Then Rosen, he gasses on about why Americans, they don't want to remember things like the fixes. He goes on about me, calls me a victim. Oh yeah. According to Rosen I'm a six-foot-six victim who made bags of cash for everybody — high school, college, bookies, sports arenas, writers like him. I brought glory to my race, he says, inspiring all these kids to try to rise like me. Selma I got to show her that. The thing I like, though, he got the names of these guys got caught like me. I forgot some.

This boy, with more talent in his fingers than most men have in their bodies, is working in a car-wash. This may well be the best job he'll ever have! And what of the others — where are they and what are they doing? Ed Warner, Herb Roth, Ed Roman, Sherman White, Nat Morgan, Ralph Beard, Lou Lipman, Mack Davis, Floyd Lane, Alex Groza, Norm Mager, Irv Dambrot and Leroy Smith — he was the one who said it, back in 1951, in his innocence and confusion: "It seems more of a business than a sport."

Oh man, I want to say, who don't know that? But Rosen, he slips my name into that list, keeps you honest. Then he says we the "few" who took the rap for the "many," goes on about how the year we all got it, 18,000 studs paid their way into Madison Square Garden for the N. I. T. championship. That was called de-emphasis, Rosen says. Brigham Young, that year they had this kid Rollie Minson, he hustled, man, they won the tournament. Rosen, he finishes with all this Holy Joe stuff.

And we're still paying our way in — and the way through college for these unknowing youths. If his value to the University is still predicated on whether he was All-City, and his scholarship figure is in proportion to his scoring, why shouldn't he still render his services and skills to the highest bidder? Let's face it, sports fans, you and I put this boy, and boys like him, in the car-wash. You and I deprived him of more than just his college education and his source of livelihood. I'll have more on this later. This is your column, too, so let me know what you think.

Hey, you in the car-wash! — What do *you* think?

You got to hand it to Rosen, when he tries, he tries. I get the column in the mail with a five dollar bill and a card, says "Taxi Fare — Be a Sport, Mack." At night at Willa's while I'm watching fat Willie drool over his clothes, he calls me. "You read my column?" he says.

"Yeah."

"So?"

"It made me cry."

He laughs, I get madder. Willie screams. Running back and forth from Willa's to home to Louie's to the Village I still got somebody tailing me. Rosen for sure —

"Look, Mack, why don't you give me a break? I'm talking to you like I'd talk to my own son. I can do something for you."

"How much?"

"I have a plan," he says. "But how can I tell it to you if you don't trust me? How can you hurt yourself, you come talk with me? Even Willa thinks it's a good idea —" He stops. "I shouldn't have told you," he says. "Look — she saw what I wrote about you and telephoned me. Do me a favor, all right? Don't tell her I told you she called." If Willa walk through the door, I'd blast her ugly puss right in, jam her teeth out the back of her neck. Who she think she is? "Let me ask you something, Mack." He's talking sly now. "Tell the truth. Are you afraid you don't have it anymore? Maybe it's easier for you this way, never testing yourself against the new boys, always thinking the way things would have been *if* you hadn't been caught. Is that it?"

"Shove it, Rosen."

"Ha! Maybe you just don't want to ever lose the stigma of the fixes — how else could you justify the way you live, the car-wash —?" He stops and I don't say nothing. "Are you there?" he asks.

"How much?" I say.

"Come, Mack," he says. "Do I approach the truth? You played the pivot, right? But you are only six-six — the boys are growing. How then would you fare against Dukes or Felix or young Chamberlain, who's past seven feet and still growing? He's at Kansas now, but he'll be in the pros soon. And what of the likes of Johnston and Arizin, Yardley or Stokes? Even old Sweetwater Clifton. The truth, Mack — could you handle them?" He sighs. "All right. I'll tell you something. You could. You were the best. But the fixes, Mack — you have to deal with them. Let me explain something to you. Sometimes we act like children when we are afraid to face things. Our sicknesses become like our toys. We don't want to give them up—"

"Save it for your column, Rosen. And don't call here again, you hear, man?"

"Did I offend you? Listen to me, Mack — I only want —" I hang up and try to get Willie quiet. I got to think. Fucken Willa, what she doing? I was right about her being in cahoots with Rosen. Next she'll be getting together with my old lady and Selma and they'll have the whole world sucking my chops to get me to improve myself. Willie, he's crying like mad and nothing I do helps, dumbass. I throw him on my shoulder and rub his back, but he keeps wailing, the mother. What everybody want from me? When Willa gets home I'm burning. I tell her a guy name of Rosen called.

"You know who he is?" I ask.

"Do I know who he is? I read him every day — him and Mary Worth, they keep me and Willie alive."

I whirl her around. "Why you call him, girl? Who you think you are?"

Bam! She gets me in the gut. "Leave off my arm, buddy," she says. "You ain't Tarzan of the jungle."

I grab her again. "Why you call him? Answer!"

"Take three guesses and don't count the first two." She grinds her knuckles into the top of my hand and I let go. "How's Willie been?"

"Ah, he's a dumb monkey," I say.

"Hey, you dumb monkey," Willa says, and she got Willie raised high in the air. "You hear what your uncle Mack call you? What you think, you ugly beautiful thing?" Willie gurgles like somebody's tickling his soul. "See — he likes being a dumb monkey, you gangling ape. Ha! Big deal! I called Rosen. So what? Why not? I got a right. You don't like it, buddy, you know what you can do."

"What?"

"Come on, come on," she says, nuzzling little Willie's neck. "Poor little Willie, ain't got no daddy. Ugly duck. You know how old Willie is? You know? He's fifteen months, going on sixteen and still can't do dick for himself. Can't walk, can't talk, can't even feed

himself. He's a prince, he is. Oh Willie, Willie —
what we gonna do with you?"

"Why you call Rosen?"

"Oh Willie, Willie," she says, holding him close and
kissing him all over. "What's gonna become of you?
What's your secret, little baby? Why you don't ever
say anything? Hey — you think maybe he's a genius?"

"A what?"

"Can't you hear? You as dumb as Willie. I said,
you think maybe he's a genius. They say kids who are
geniuses don't talk as quick as others. Einstein, they
thought he was a moron. You take psychology when
you was at school?"

"No."

"Au-tistic — you know what that is? Au-tistic children, I read about them in *The Star*. It's psychology.
When a kid's mixed up inside and don't say or do
nothing at all, then he's *au*-tistic. Means he's got
violence somewhere in him. Hey Willie love, you got
violence in you? You gonna take after Mack with a
carving knife, huh? Ha! Maybe it wasn't au-tistic —
maybe it was *ar*-tistic! Willie look like an artist to
you?"

"Why you call Rosen?"

"Oh man, come off it, huh?" she says. "That all you
can think about? Grow up, babe. Grow up."

"Just tell me why, that's all," I say.

She jabs her finger at my chest. "Listen, buddy,
I don't got to tell you anything I don't want to. Why
I call him? You know as well as me. You don't want

to talk to him, nobody can make you. You're a big boy, Mack. You don't have to do anything you don't want to. That includes staying here."

"Meaning?"

"That door's got two sides to it, you look careful."

"You're damn right," I say, but before I got the door open all the way she's hanging on my neck, cutting my breath. I grab her wrists, but, man, she's got the power! Her armbone, it's under my adam's apple. Then she got a leg behind my knee and crash! I'm on the floor and she's flying on top of me, screaming like a maniac. I cover my face, try to take deep breaths and all of a sudden she's flush on me, her mouth at my ear, laughing like hell with her fingers working my ribs. Then I'm laughing too. "You're out of your box, girl," I say.

"Ain't I though!" she says.

Fat Willie, he's banging on the side of his crib, laughing. Oh yeah, he's a genius. Him and me.

Later me and Willa talk some. She's good to talk to. She knows what I'm thinking sometimes.

Okay. What I got to lose? She don't mention Rosen again, but I say I'll go see him. Not to her. But I make up my mind. Maybe it'll get him off my back. I got to get finished with this thing, that's for sure.

I get to work in the morning and they got surprises for me. Oh yeah. Rosen, he's heading me straight for the big-time. Old Smokey, he's so dumb drunk he can hardly stand, he keeps giggling all day. I tell him not to breathe so hard on the cars, he's gonna melt the paint off. The other guys, they all know something, but don't say nothing. Ha! I'm getting like Willa, huh? talking like that. I got to remember that for her. They all know something, but don't say nothing, they're old car-washers, just keep mopping along. I tell it to myself a couple of times and its getting less and less funny when they break the news to me. Louie, he calls me over and puts his arm around me like I'm his regular ass-hole buddy. He's short and fat too. The whole world's gonna wind up being penguins, they don't watch out. Louie, he's got Rosen's column under his arm, his ugly puss grinning at you, and Smokey and the guys they crowd around. Then they all start jabbering, saying they put two and two together, and the next thing I know they're presenting me with this cotton T-shirt and shorts, in gold and blue, says *Louie's Leapers* on it, the shirt.

"How you like that?" Smokey says. "The name! That's my idea. Not bad, huh? You got to say so, don't you, guys? Not bad. I'm a dribbling fool. Watch my gas!" Then he grabs a hat off Jim, a guy about my age who never says anything, and they all playing saloogie around him with it like a bunch of kids. "I've always wanted to sponsor an athletic team," Louie's saying, his arm still around my waist. "Every year kids from the neighborhood come to me, asking for money for uniforms for baseball teams, for basketball teams. I had a bowling team once — before you started here, Mack, but it did so poorly I became discouraged. With you playing for us, though, it is a different story. We can go places, I'm sure." He calls to me with his pudgy finger and I bend down toward him. "Listen — if you do well, maybe there'll be an extra little gift in your pay envelope once in a while."

Then he stands up proud. "How much?" I say.

He laughs. "You're all right, Mack boy," he says. "I know I can depend on you." He's babbling on, I'm not sure I can follow what's happening. The guys are still running all around me like a bunch of loons. Man, the whole world's cracking up. "Now Jim Wilson played basketball at Manual Training High School. And Smokey claims that when he is not as he puts it — *into* the influence — he can play. Johnson there is old, but he is built like a *bulvan!* Under the boards, who would fight with him? You can have a team, Mack! Over there, on the side of the quonset hut, I've ordered a backboard from a sporting goods firm. We'll put it up. You have a lot of time during the day when cars are not coming in, you can practice." A car honks and the guys break up their game. I move toward the car but Louie pulls me back.

"Hey there, Goose Tatum!" Smokey calls to me. "You rest up yourself. We don't want to overwork our stars when we only got one." So the guys move the car into the booth and Louie keeps talking. "Now about the league we're in, Mack. It's sponsored by the B'nai B'rith, but it's non-sectarian, so you shouldn't have any qualms because of your race or religion." He keeps gassing me about the league and the number of games and the teams and how the head of his Jewish Center thinks it's a great idea too. That Rosen, he really start something, man, looks like he leave me to finish it. Oh yeah, I think, that guy McCarthy still prowling around

the country the way he was when I got caught, I get
him to go snooping after Rosen's drawers. After the
judge got finished with me, used to stay home days,
watching McCarthy on TV, he's real mean on offense,
he do the job on Rosen. "The director, do you know
what he said I was? He told me I am a community-
directed man!" Oh man, he just don't want to stop
talking. My arms long enough, I stretch them, get
that director guy too. "As for what happened to you,
Mack, I say — let bygones be bygones. Live and let
live. But — and don't misunderstand me — I took the
precaution of checking with the executive director,
just to be sure, and he said the same thing. 'Louis,' he
said to me, 'we are not a people to condemn a man
for a single unfortunate error.' He said that, and he
reminded me of the three cities of refuge in the Bible.
'It's a Jewish concept," he said." Then he gasses about
the Bible for a while and man, I'm ready to bust my
skin, he got me so tight. Why? I want to slug him,
the guys too when they come back around and start
patting my ass and rubbing my arms and telling me
how great I am. They all bore me, is the truth. They
fucken bore me so much I'm like to die listening to
them. Oh yeah, I'm bored, man. Who I fooling?
Louie's Leapers, we gonna be the scourge of the
eastern seaboard, us. Oh yeah. We get through, the
Harlem Globetrotters gonna have to go back to Africa.
Make way for us, babes. We're black and we're beautiful! "Only one favor I have to ask of you, Mack,"
Louie says. "Now don't get me wrong, if it's not an
acceptable proposition to you, I'll forget it; but I have

a nephew who is sports-crazy. Sports, sports, sports—
that's all he ever thinks about. At camp last summer
he won a big award. Do you think you could let him
play with us? It would be a favor to me. My wife
and her sister, they wouldn't understand if I had a
team and I couldn't let my own nephew play on it.
Now, mind you, he's not a bad ballplayer —"

"Sure," I say. "We'll just rub a little shine on his
face and he be one of us — right, boys?" The guys
laugh at this. I don't got to say much to get them to
laugh. That's what being a hero means. It's a great
life. Oh yeah. Willa, she gonna split her ass laughing
at me — king of the Minit-wash. Next year, who
knows? Maybe fat Julie, if he don't croak, he'll even
talk to me again. Ronnie, when I get through, he can
step right into my shoes. That is, they don't retire my
uniform number. Oh yeah, I'm so excited, I don't
know if I can make it through the rest of the day
waiting to break the news to my mother and father.

Trouble is, I keep thinking about what was. You
ever pick a dime off the top of a backboard? You do
that, you've made it, man. In the pros, there's not
more than a few guys can do it, all of them six-ten or
over. In the schoolyard, I wasn't even out of high
school yet, still had all these scouts and coaches breathing down my ass, I did it the first time. Big Ed, they
boosted him up on someone's shoulders to put it there,
then all the guys cheered me on. Took me three shots,
but I made it. Oh man, I was king then. I mean, you
make it big-time — high school, college, pro, I don't
care where, it never compares with being king of your

own schoolyard. You can take all the fame and shove it; when I walk through the gates and the guys are sitting along the fence, younger guys, and they say "Hi, Mack!" or "Hey, Mack babe — you want next with me?" and I see this look in their eyes like they'd give their right balls to be me, man, that's all I need. I'm home free. The Penguin, he got a ladder before our game against Duke and he put a dime up and the stands, thousands, went out of their boxes when I aced up and snatched the mother, but it don't compare, I tell you. Why's that? Oh yeah. I get to thinking. You get out there when you're young, on a sunny day, and you listen to the older guys gas with each other about who's got what shots and what moves and who can fake who out of whose jock, and you just ache to have them talk to you. Shit, you get brought up in a white boy's schoolyard, hear them argue for years about every ballplayer ever was — I mean, they know 'em all and can quote you figures, babe — you can't help let it get to you. When you play out there, you're loose, too. When I sail up there and snatch that dime that first time, man, that was the high spot. I could of died right then, I die happy. I think about that lots. I wonder if I can still do it. Not with my pot, though. Goddamn Louie, why I have to take his gas? Why I can't just tell him to take his team and take his uniforms and take his Jewboys and shove them all? Oh Mack, you poor mother, you sure losing your brash. Time was, you called the plays and made the moves.

By the time I'm ready to check out I've been thinking too much about what it be like to play again. Oh

Mack, you dumbass, I say, why you can't resist? Your ass dragging over the hill already, but you looking to float up there and sail over everybody, pick that dime off again. What that gonna prove? You be lucky you don't get your ass handed to you by some young sharpie. Then he be telling everybody in his school-yard how he outscore, outplay, outrebound, outevery-thing the great Mack Davis. Oh yeah. You be lucky Louie don't bench you. He waves at me goodby, I go up to him. "About that team," I say. "I'll let you know — okay, man?"

"What do you mean?" he asks, and I know I got him where I want. Okay, Mack, you wheeling and dealing now.

"I mean I'll let you know if I want to play. I got more to do with my nights than run around some band-box gym with a bunch of high school kids."

"But this is a superior league, Mack," he says. "I wouldn't enter us if not. The teams have many former college players on them."

"Still, I'll let you know. Okay?"

His jaw about ready to hit the floor. "But I've ordered all the uniforms!"

I shrug. "I didn't tell you to. I mean, I don't play, maybe you can still get up a team. Make your nephew captain. Maybe he got some friends."

He laughs. "Don't kid with me like this, Mack."

"Who's kidding?"

"But I've promised the Center — I've told every-body —"

"Well, I'll let you know," I say and walk off. He

waddles after me, touches my arm. I turn around.

"Look, Mack, haven't I treated you well here?"

"Sure," I say, pat him on the shoulder. "You're a swell boss, Louie."

"You will play then, won't you?"

"Look, I said I'll let you know! I got to think it over, man. I got to consider things, like — I run around and advertise your business and what's in it for me? You know what I mean? I don't need no more uniforms —"

He lets out a big thing of air and draws his height up. "All right," he says, "I will make a deal with you. Five dollars a game — cash, so you won't have to declare for taxes."

I laugh so hard at this he's about to fall over backwards from my wind. "Louie," I say, bending over, my arm around his shoulder. "You're a real businessman, you are!"

Then I'm gone, when he calls this time I don't turn around. I'm feeling all right again. Okay, Rosen, here I come!

FOUR

ON THE WAY I get to laughing at Louie and thinking. Five spots a game. Oh man, I'm making it. Yeah. Me and Jim Thorpe. I remember in the movies, Burt Lancaster, he was Thorpe, and he winds up his life playing for half-assed football teams at ten bucks a game. He's over the hill and been drinking and his kid died and his wife's left him. And he never gets his Olympic medals back. He plays Indian chiefs in carnivals too. I figure, me too, things get bad enough. Yeah, me and Thorpe, we do war dances together, we be the only real Americans left. What a screw he got. Just because he took fifteen bucks once for expenses for this semi-pro baseball team. I mean, he got nothing on me. Only thing gets me, is how come he care so much about those medals? Show you how dumb an Indian can be. What'd he think? People giving him medals and telling him he was the greatest because they love his ass? Man, you stop producing, you lucky they don't take your pants from you. Shit, he pretty dumb, for all the work he did, only getting a bunch of medals. Guess things were different then. Yeah. Ten bucks for bumping heads on a football field when he was past forty. But I think: if Thorpe can get ten for busting his chops way back in 1930 I can get more than five from Louie. The depression's over, man.

Rosen, he got bigger plans. I walk inside his apartment and first thing I know he's sitting me down, giving me a drink and showing me this thing he got typed up. "It's for tomorrow's column. Maybe. What do you think?" He's so excited, like a little kid. "You just relax and read it and I'll fix us some sandwiches. You like hot pastrami?"

"Sure."

"On rye or whole wheat?"

"Rye."

"I'll put a little mustard on too." When he looks at me his eyes so happy, I squirm. Then he goes into the kitchen and leaves me alone. His column's on this cheap yellow paper, typed.

YOU REMEMBERED, ALL RIGHT!

By Ben Rosen

I was gratified to have so many of you respond to my column last week about the basketball fixes. Your response proves that you do remember them. "Big deal," writes Morris X from the Bronx. "So a bunch of crooks got caught. They may have your sympathy, but they don't have mine. Why should I care about a bunch of kids who sold out? They got what they deserved!" Morris, you are in good company. Perhaps you would be interested in what Nat Holman said in 1951 when his C. C. N. Y. boys were booked: "We must keep going. The game has meant too much to the youth of the college, the nation, even the world, to be affected by half a dozen kids with a price."

Then Rosen, he goes on about how they forged high school and college records for guys at C. C. N. Y., drags up all this stuff from the fixes, it be better he leave it dead, you ask me. He got the facts, though. These other cats write in to him, he can quote you things.

Judge Streit, you may recall, was the first judge to hand out sentences to the gamblers and the fixers. "The responsibility," he said in December of 1951, "must be shared not only by the crooked fixers and the corrupt players, but also by the college administrations, coaches and alumni . . . the naïveté, the equivocation and denials of the coaches and their assistants concerning their knowledge of gambling, recruiting and subsidizing would be comical were they not so despicable."

Such statements do not need rebuttals from you or me. In 1951, Matty Bell, athletic director at Southern Methodist University (where, in 1951, they gave out 154 athletic scholarships — and 152 academic scholarships) reacted to the above speech. "It isn't any of the judge's business," he declared. "What of it?" said Dr. Harry "Curly" Byrd, then President of the University of Maryland.

Rosen got more stories for you than that. The guy I like best, though, he's the President of Bradley University. Two guys on his team, after all he does for them, this Judge Streit gets to preach to them too.

And this, after President Owen had accompanied the basketball team to every away game, had allowed the local Boosters Club to give money to his ballplayers, and had, when a player came to him for advice, told his star that he should not answer a subpoena in a murder case (the star was a witness) because it conflicted with a basketball game!

I cut through the rest of the column, get to the bottom, Rosen got this thing he has sometimes, what happened five years ago. I like that.

FIVE YEARS AGO THIS WEEK: While Senator Joe McCarthy was going to court for slugging Drew Pearson, Allie Reynolds pitched his second no-hitter of the year . . . Ferris Fain was leading the American League in batting with a .344 average . . . Preacher Roe (22–3) and Bob Feller (22–8) led the majors in pitching . . . in Brooklyn, Harry Gross, Bookie Extraordinaire, refused to testify against 21 cops . . . Dave Koslo won a big game as the Giants closed in on the fading Dodgers.

Five years ago. Oh yeah, that McCarthy can't do the job maybe I get that cat Kefauver you always seeing on TV, investigating everybody. Now that Tricky Dick beat him, we get him to work on Rosen, ship him out of the country like he did Frank Costello. Rosen, he sees I'm done.

"So?" he says.

"So what?"

"All right, all right, be that way," he says. Then he smiles. "Here. Here's your pastrami sandwich. There's more mustard if you want." Then he leans back and chews his sandwich like a contented moron. "I'm going to ask you some questions in a minute and I want you to answer as best you can. Feel free with

me, Mack. Just say whatever comes into your head."
When I eat I remember how hungry I am. "Just talk
to me the way you would to a friend. What we say
to each other is in the strictest of confidence. So feel
free. Begin where you want —"

He takes a pencil out of his side pocket, then he
smiles at me. What I supposed to do? Fucken Willa!
That Kefauver, he ship her out too. I never should of
come. I look at Rosen and he looks at me. I look
down, then up and he's still grinning. Man, we can't
stay here like this all night. "I got nothing to say,"
I say.

"But you came here, Mack. You must want to tell
me something. You may not think it's important, but
tell me anyway. What harm can there be in that?"

"What's your game, Rosen?"

"Game? What makes you think I have a game? Do
you think everybody in the world has an angle? That
everybody is trying to use you?"

"Enough questions, buddy," I say, standing up.

"Do my questions bother you?" I look at the wall.
There's a picture of Rosen when he's young. You can
tell it's him by the nose and the stupid grin. He's
standing with this baseball player in the steps of a
dugout. "That was the great Moe Berg," Rosen says.
"Moe played for the Dodgers before you were born.
He is a lawyer now. That picture was taken when
he first came up with the Dodgers — straight from
Princeton to Ebbets Field. He could speak seven
languages then —" I walk away from the picture.

"What are you so restless about?" Rosen asks. "Are you annoyed about something? Tell me, Mack. Tell me."

I can't take it no more. I jerk him from his chair and his pencil and pad spill off. I pull his face close to mine and his breath stinks. I got him by the collar and he's still smiling, mustard on his bottom lip, only his face gets red real quick and I drop him down. He got a lot of little lines around his mouth and eyes like my old man. What good it do to slug him?

"Ah, I thought so!" he says. "You're angry with me, aren't you?"

I walk around the room, not saying. He gets out of his chair and comes to me. He's breathing hard from being scared. "The truth, Mack?" he whispers. "You'd like revenge, wouldn't you?" His eyes are shining. "You wanted to kill me, didn't you?"

"Nah."

"All right, you didn't *want* to — but your anger, it made you want to kick my face in, am I not right? To slug me, bash me, mutilate me! Tell the truth, Mack. The things I remind you of — the fixes, the college, big-time athletics — they all stir in you a fearful desire, a confused need. The truth, Mack, wouldn't you like to get even with somebody? Maybe one of the gamblers — or your coach — somebody who started you in the whole thing. Who, Mack?"

"Nobody."

The light leaves his eyes and he sits down again, I do too. "Well," he says, then again, "Well." He laughs, more to himself than to me. "Well, maybe it is me you would like to kill, to murder — for reminding you."

"Look," I say. "I told you before. I got nobody to blame for anything. I do what I want. Nobody ever made me do anything. That clear?"

"And the only thing you are sorry about is that they turned the money off —"

"That's right."

"Good," he says. "We are getting somewhere." He fixes himself in his chair. "Well." He picks a pair of glasses off the table next to him and puts them on. First time I see him with four-eyes and it makes him look older. Man, what's going on, I almost beat up an old man? "Well, let us start from the beginning again. All right? My columns, what did you think of them?"

"I told you. They made me cry."

"Yes." He chews on his pencil, then points it at me. "But aren't you interested, say, in what has become of all the others? Of Warner and Roman and White?"

"They can look out for themselves," I say. "Anyway, I know about some of them. They play in the Eastern league, in Jersey, most of them."

"Who, for example?"

"White and — ah, what's the difference?" I shrug. "Some guys offered me jobs playing there. I did it a few times. Got twenty-five bucks a game."

"So why did you stop?"

I shrug. "Too much trouble for twenty-five bucks. Didn't get home till late and had to get up the next day for work. I don't know," I say. "It just bugged

me, playing with all these guys." Inside, I got to laugh.
I thought that was bad and here I am, gonna be the
star of *Louie's Leapers*. Oh yeah. I'm making progress, me.

"I see," he says. "But you don't, I take it, keep in
touch with the others?"

"What you think, man, we got a club?" I got to
laugh. "Oh yeah. The Fixer's Alumni Association,
that's us. We get together and gas about old times
gone. We compare notes on dumped games, gamblers
we worked with, judges we stood before. That's good,
Rosen. Don't you think?"

He laughs too. "You're all right, Mack. All right.
Only — only," he leans forward, "don't resist me so
much. When you were laughing now — wasn't that
better?" Then he's up out of his chair standing over
me, his hand out. "Let us be friends," he says. "And
try not to quarrel. I will try not to — to bug you, and
you, please try to be a little patient with me, all right?
Clasp my hand." I look at him like he's crazy. "Why
not?" he says. What I got to lose, I say. I shake his
hand and he puts his left one on top of mine, his
hands are warm. "Just one thing I ask of you," he says,
still holding my hand in his paw. "You see, I have a
daughter and if she should come here and meet you
—" His face is straight, then when he sees the question
on mine, it breaks and he slaps his hands. He roars,
cackles like a machine gun and I got to laugh too,
seeing how he had me fooled. "And I'll tell my son
not to marry your daughter, all right? Then we'll
have a real marriage contract —" He can't stop laugh-

ing. Seems stupid to me but watching his eggplant body shake, him wiping the tears from his eyes, I got to laugh too. "Listen to me carefully," he says when he's stopped. He got a bunch of newspaper clippings on his lap. "My research," he explains. "I have been going through the newspapers of five years ago for background material. What a time that was, Mack! Do you remember?" He waves at me. "Of course you do. McCarthy was running around the country, our boys getting killed in Korea, fixers and gamblers — it's all here. Marciano beating Louis, DiMaggio retiring. General MacArthur defying the President, Frank Costello and the Rosenbergs, Sobell and Virginia Hill — there are stories. There are stories. But Ernie Nemeth is the important man of that era. Do you remember Ernie Nemeth?"

"No."

"All right, then. I will tell you about Ernie Nemeth. Listen carefully. Five years ago this week, Ernie Nemeth was the most important man in America, but he has been forgotten." He leans back and makes a tent with his fingertips. "Five years ago this week, Ernie Nemeth went to court with a case that had no precedent and, until now, has had no imitator. Here. Ernie Nemeth played football for the University of Denver. That was his job. For this, they gave him the status of a college student. They paid for his education and, in addition, gave him a salary of twenty-six dollars a week, which supposedly went for a campus job. Now Ernie Nemeth was injured in spring practice and could not play football for the University of

Denver, so the University took away his job and his twenty-six dollars a week. What did Ernie Nemeth do? He found himself a lawyer who had Ernie apply for Workmen's Compensation, listing Ernie's job as "Football Player." But the state would not give Ernie his money because they claimed that college football was a game. Ernie Nemeth's lawyer, a Mr. Lowy, went to court with his case — and the judge awarded young Ernie thirteen dollars a week, to be paid from the time of injury until he could return to his job! There —!"

"So?"

"So?" he says. "So don't you see!"

"See what?"

"Ah, Mack, Mack. The court of the state of Denver recognized that playing sports for a college is a *job!* Don't you see what that means? How much did the college give you when you were there?"

"The usual — a free ride plus sixty a month for laundry."

"That was all? Come, Mack. A star like you — what else?"

"That's my business."

"All right. One question only — did you have a job?"

"Yeah, sweeping out the gym."

"How much?"

"I got a check of one-fifteen a month from the athletic department for that." I got to laugh. "Never did it, either. They had janitors. I used to pick up a broom once a week and sweep off the foul line, make a production of it, the guys on the team used to kid around about it."

"And when you were implicated in point-fixing, did they take away your job?"

"Yeah."

"See!" he says. "Think of all the others, Mack. Not only the fixers like yourself, but all the boys with injuries — like Ernie Nemeth. Do you realize how much money the states owe all of you boys?"

"You're off your nut, Rosen," I say. "Okay, so some smart lawyer got this Nemeth cat some money. Good for him. But, man, how you gonna collect *back* money? I know something about being unemployed; you got to show up right away, you lose your job, and you got to keep showing up and making believe you're looking for new jobs. Anyway, I wasn't injured. Like I was kicked out of school, man! Like they suspended me. Like they didn't want no fixers going to classes at their holy church." I'm standing up now, over him. "So what you want with me? You want to go to court, get publicity, you get yourself another stooge, you hear, man?"

"Easy, Mack," he says. "Easy. You want something to drink? Beer perhaps? I have Schaefers. Or maybe something hard. Scotch? Rye? Or a Coca-Cola?"

"I got to go," I say. He's next to me, leaning on my arm.

"Look," he says, "before I forget, I have something for you. For your part of our project." He works through stuff on his desk, finds what he wants. It's an envelope, my name typed on the front. He gives it to me. "Open it," he says. "Don't be afraid." I do, inside are two tens and a five. "What's this for?" I ask. "For you — for your story. Now, don't think because you accept the money that you're obligated to me in any way. You've more than fulfilled your part of the bargain by listening to my nonsense for this long. The beer — you want some?"

"Sure. Why not?"

He's back in a second, beer fizzing out over the top of the can. "Put the money away," he says. "It's yours. Cash, so you don't have to report it for tax purposes —" I start to laugh, slow at first. "And also to show you my faith." I'm laughing harder now. "For I could issue a check and have it stopped at the bank." Louie and Rosen, between them I'm gonna be rich yet. "What's so funny?" Oh man, this is too much. Jim Thorpe, yeah, he had nothing on me. This Ernie Nemeth too, only thirteen a week, I got to laugh. Reminds me of college. Yeah. Money used to turn up there like dead bodies in a Charlie Chan movie. It started before I ever got to college. These checks would come in the mail — they'd be bank checks with no signatures for travel expenses visiting these colleges. Always more. Got fifty to go into the city to visit the coach of this New York college. Pretty good profit there. And airplane tickets come my way, even gift certificates to Brooks Brothers. What I want with that? Gave that to my old lady and she got the money for it somehow. Leave it to her. But at the university, that's where I did okay. Oh yeah. I had market value, man. Goldstein, my high school coach, he counted up and I had forty-seven colleges come sniffing after my drawers. Goldstein, he did okay too. He'd tell the alumni or whoever it was that he'd put in a good word to me about the spook's college, and the guy would slip Goldstein some juice. I knew. When they had me down in their office in the field house, all of them telling me how I wouldn't regret signing up with them, and after they'd promised me the works — tuition, room, board, laundry money, a scholarship for the Penguin, travel money for flying home vacation, and hints at some other long green would be coming my way if I scored my load and turned out to be the ball-player they thought I was — then I put the screws on. "It was real nice of you guys to give me the plane money to come out here," I said to them, "but the thing is, see, I got this car I was expecting to take to school here next fall when I come. "Well, that's fine," they said, going on about how freshmen weren't al-lowed to have cars on campus but they'd get me a permit anyway if I promised not to get into trouble. "Thanks," I said, "only the thing is I still got these payments on the car, see? I mean, if I don't pay off these payments the company gonna come and take my car away and then how I gonna come out here and be an All-American for you nice gentlemen?" They looked at each other then and I blinked my eyes, innocent me, and they knew the score. "How much?" they asked. "Seven hundred fifty three dollars and ninety seven cents," I said, snatching a figure out of the sky. "Too much," the athletic director said, I shrugged and stood up, looking down on him. "I guess maybe I'll have to go to one of them schools in New York City where I can live at home. You know how much money I could save living at home? And there's this college there, they said if I take their scholarship, they get my old man a job. He don't work, you know. At this job, he still don't work much, but it be more income for my folks than from the government." Then I spin on to them about how they gonna give me room and board money if I live with my folks and by the time I get through, man, we even got a scholarship set up for Selma when she gets ready to go to college. Only her, they won't need to phony no records for her, I tell them. What I score in basketball she gets on tests. Her and Ronnie, they got the brains. I work hard for my money too, leading the freshman team in scoring, rebounding and everytime I turn around, they thanking me. This clothing store in town, they send me a charge account, tell me it's the gift of a friend. Same with all the restaurants and movies. Next year, when I'm varsity, somebody open a bank account in my name. How you like that? That thing come in the mail at my dormitory, I about to piss green. First game I play, I score seventeen points and that bank account got seventeen dollars in it. When they forget to fill it up, I remind them. Oh yeah, money, it turns up everywhere. And Big Ed, I tell him about it, he just pats me on the back and says "I told you so." When money stop coming in fast, I make a little trip to the athletic office and tell them about these coaches and alumni from other colleges keep calling me and asking if I'm happy here. I say, "How come they want to know if I'm happy? I just can't understand it. I mean, after they paid my way to visit their schools and took me out to eat and spent all that time on me, man, you'd think they wouldn't ever give a shit what happened to me. But they keep coming around, asking if I'm happy here. What you think I should say to them?" And the athletic director, "Tank" Warfield's his name, was an All-American guard in football, he always gives me that look and I always blink my eyes and the next thing I know some alumni's writing out a check so I can buy schoolbooks. Got to send money home too, for my ailing father and my hardworking mother. And Selma, she got to see how she likes the school so they pay for her to come out and visit me. I take her into the athletic office, I remember, she looking real pretty in this lavender suit she bought special to come out, and I say to Warfield, "There's your next scholarship student," and he says, "Well, we'll see about that —" and I jab my finger in his beerbelly and say, "We'll see nothing. You promised she'd get a free ride here too. You keep your word, man, or you find your basketball team sweeping the cellar of your precious league." "Sure, Mack," he says. "But don't push us too far." This the one time I respect him, cause he tells the truth. "Remember who you are," and he's jabbing my chest now. "You're just another jig ballplayer. There's more like you in every schoolyard in New York." Selma, she pulls my arm to go, she never does like the scholarship business. Not for my mother, she wouldn't have said she take it someday. "Yeah, but you got an investment

in me," I say. "Your face look pretty red, I up and
quit now. Man, there'd be a lot of alumni screaming
for your scalp we don't go to a tournament this year.
Your football team hurting enough as is, all you got
left is me, buddy. You remember that." He's piss mad
now and I laugh at him. "Okay," he says. "We both
know the score. But we got a freshman as good as you
coming up next year. Then you're dispensable, Mack.
Without our help, you'll be flunked out of this place
so fast you won't know what hit you. So you play ball
with us, we play ball with you, got it? You've got no
kicks coming. We've treated you fair and square."
He's right. I got no kicks coming. They pluck me out
of the schoolyard like the witch does Cinderella. And
all the white meat I'm pronging, they got more trouble
from me they know how to handle. "McKee's a good
coach. You get the boot now, we'd still have a respect-
able season, so you just know your place a little
more." He's bluffing same as me — we both caught
like brother fish — but he's right, you bite the hand
that feed you long enough, it take away the power. I
put my arm around his shoulder. "Just teasing, Tank,"
I say to him, and wink. "You ain't mad, are you,
man? Just trying to show off for my beautiful sister,
you know?" "Sure," he says. "She's a good looking
kid. Maybe she'll be a cheerleader someday. One of
the cheerleaders this year is a Negro girl." "Hey, what
you think of that, Selma?" I say. "Can you dream of
anything you'd rather be? Oh man, you be queen of
this whole place, have every guy eating out of your
hand." Selma, she look bashful a second, then her

jaw set and I know I go too far with her too. She only sixteen then, but she knows the difference between things. Not too much you can fool her with. "No hard feelings, huh, Tank? You watch my gas against Illinois this week. If I don't score twenty you can have my jock." Score twenty-eight that game. I ain't so smart, though. They give me the money for the car, but the quarterback on the football team, he's got a brand new job. Big Ed, I tell him, he says there's ways of getting money for my own car. I remember: in the school-yard before, before I'm even on the team at Erasmus he brings down copies of magazines, *Sport* and *Life* and *Look,* and he shows me pictures of these ball-players with their big cars and homes. "They're all yours someday, Mack, you play your hand right," he says. "How'd you like to have one of those?" he says pointing to a sleek Caddy. "Or give your mother a refrigerator like that? Or wear clothes like that? And have babes like that creaming over you?" He shows me guys dressed up to kill, stepping into restaurants and out of cabs and eating big meals and playing golf and getting TV sets from fans who love them. Then he gets me on the court and bangs me around. No-body rougher than Big Ed under the boards, he uses his ass, man. Cant move him. Time goes by, I fly over him, but he times things and bounces me when he wants. I show him too much of the ball he makes me eat it. Quick hands. Can't figure then how come he can't make it big-time. Once he takes me to see the Knicks — that's before I'm on the team and have my own pass into the Garden — and "Tricky Dick"

McGuire, he's like Ed, passing two-handed, looking one way, hitting a man cutting the other way. Zoom! That ball goes when he passes it, spins like hell. He teaches me to go to my left well as my right. Sometimes I meet him in the schoolyard when he's done working and it's getting dark and he works me, makes me go either way, hook righty, lefty, dribble to both sides, fake either way, go up right and switch mid-air to left. He teaches me position. Keeps showing me magazines, too. College ballplayers in front of these ivy buildings, sitting in convertibles with their girl-friends. Doak Walker. I remember him. Good looking stud. And Charley Justice and Charlie Trippi and this guy who played the accordion, Tony Lavelli. Always with books under their arms and these V-necked sweaters and these smiling blond chicks cream-ing over their dicks. Yeah. So I'm not that smart, only getting what I did. Not so smart getting caught, either. Selma, she wouldn't say nothing then, but she didn't like it either. We had good times, though. Fixed her up with the freshman ballplayer the Tank talked about. D. A. got him too, before he ever played a varsity game, just for taking some gifts from this guy, didn't even rig a game yet. We went to a dance together and Selma, she the prettiest one there. We talked a lot afterwards and when I got home at vaca-tion, she kept thanking me. Took her to class and to the dance and just walking around the campus intro-ducing her to everybody. Felt pretty good. Big Ed, he come out to see me play in the fieldhouse a few times before he put me in on the goods. It's after the

first year and I'm home on vacation and he asks me
how I'm making it. I say okay, how you making it?
But I don't got to ask. He's dressed sharp, I remember.
I've got four or five inches on him by then, but not
around the middle. He's getting bigger, puffing on a
cigar, without his sneakers. Says he's getting too old
to run around a schoolyard. I tell him he looks like
somebody's studding him, he laughs. "How's your
folks?" he asks. "Getting along," I say. "Look," he
says, getting down to business. "You're doing okay at
college now, Mack. You're king out there. They give
you some pocket money, you get a free ride, you
finish four years maybe you got a little bankroll tucked
away. But how long's it gonna last? And how much?
A thousand? Two thousand? And I'm quoting gen-
erous figures to you, right? You're a good kid, Mack.
You're probably giving a lot of what you make to your
folks, right? Okay. So let's say you save a little and
you make the pros. You'll make it, we don't got to
worry about that. So unless you're a Mikan or a Cousy,
how much you gonna make? Ten-fifteen grand a year
if you're lucky. You get married, have some kids, how
much you gonna have left? All of a sudden you're
thirty years old and some hotshots are making you
look silly on that court. Then what? Listen to me,
boy, these are your productive years! You put something away now, you can build yourself a future. Hell,
that university, they take in more in one game with
you playing than you'll make in five years, right?
What do you get for it? Gamblers, they make thousands betting on you — what do you get out of it?

Shit, that's what. A minor league salary. There's guys
come down to this schoolyard, they make more money
just betting on your games than you do playing. Take
me — I'll tell you the truth now — this year, when
Kentucky played DePaul I made fifteen hundred dollars. I'm not shitting you. I had DePaul and ten points.
Kentucky won by eight." Then he looks around and
tells me what he's been leading to. "That's just one
game. Mack, so help me God, I made over forty
thousand this year on games! And I'm small fry. If
I had big money to put down — I'd own Madison
Square Garden by now." Then he tells me how the
whole thing works, how players, All-Americans then,
they keep winning, but they just stay inside the point
spreads. They're favored to win by eleven, they win
by ten. And he tells me how they do it. The tricks.
It's a snap. "Don't be a sucker," he says. "If you were
a white boy, you'd have a big car, more money, everything — don't let 'em use you, Mack. The next three
years are investment years. You play it right, you be
set for a long long time. Then you're free to play how
you want." He stops then, I remember. We're watching the guys playing ball and there's this backcourt
man, he's got hands! Goes up for a shot and before
you know it, two men on him, he's passed off to a free
man under the basket. Swish! "We been pretty good
pals a long time, Mack, I don't want anything I say
or do to interfere with that, you hear? I mean that.
As much as I ever meant anything. So if you don't
like what I'm saying to you, we both just make believe
this conversation never took place, that clear?" I

swear to God, he got tears in his eyes. "You're like a fucken brother to me," he says. "Special. And no rule of the schoolyard says you got to play it my way. You got different ideas — I don't care what they are — you just tell me to take my suitcase and go peddling at some other guy's door, okay? So you think it over, what I've been saying. You let me know whenever you want and I'll put you in touch with the right guys. You got all summer, all fall, even after the season starts next year." "Shit, man," I say to him. "What's there to think on? I got a long future, needs a big invest-ment. What I got to do?" Then he's pounding me on the back and we're pumping hands up and down and he's going on about how smart I am, and how I'll never regret my decision, and then, shoes and shirt and tie and all, him and me play next together with some little kid and we whiz through all-comers, until Big Ed, he's about to collapse. Goddamn them all. Where is he now? Penguin says he's at home, never goes out since he got out of jail, just gets heavier and heavier. Had two heart attacks already. Once, he says, once the guys say he came down to the schoolyard, looking as wide as a house, his face so full of flab you could hardly recognize him, it spread his features so, just stood back next to the fence watching the guys play. Rosen, he's still blabbing on, God knows about what.

"All right," I hear from far. "You won't answer that, let me ask you something else. What schoolyard do you play in, Mack?"

"What?"

"Come," he says. "You can't fool an old-timer like

me. What schoolyard? Every basketball player, be he the world's best or the world's worst, lives for his schoolyard. It's where he grows, where he lives out his youth, where he finds his glory. Maybe not for you as much as for my generation. For us it was an Eden! I remember when I was younger, waiting two hours sometimes for a next, just to play with the older players, the stars. Come, Mack. Tell me. On weekends, where do you play? Maybe I could come down, take some pictures of you — then we put them side by side with pictures of you in the N.C.A.A. tournament — then and now!"

I just look at him some, now knowing what to answer. Man, it's like he's tuned in on me. I think of the schoolyard, I remember every crack in the ground. The ridge under the backboard where if the ball hits it goes off at a crazy angle, the diamonds of the wire fence where I hung my sweatshirt, squeezing it next to the metal bar. Oh yeah. Rosen, he got me where he wants if he knows it, got my number, dumbass me. Something's going off in my head, ringing. What they trying to do to me? Him, Willa, Julie, Big Ed, Ronnie, Louie — what they want from me? They had this dead spot on the backboard, right side, you like to throw the ball through that spot, it just curl into the basket easy, any angle. Remember when they tore up the concrete way back and took the pole out, put these two new jobbers in, set back from the court, so you don't bust your teeth driving in.

Rosen, he's still talking, only not to me. Something wet. Shit. Beercan tipped in my lap, dripping onto my hand, I turn it up straight. The ringing, Rosen, he's on the phone. "The check? . . . no, I didn't forget, you'll have it in the mail . . ." I drink some more and look around the room, feel restless, bones itching. There's a few autographed balls on the table with his typewriter. "Of course I want to talk to my son . . ." His voice changes. "Say hey, champ! — how goes it? . . . Are you squeezing that rubber ball the way I told you? . . . Good, it builds up your wrist muscles . . . hey, don't forget, we have a date . . . a week from Saturday at Baker Field, Columbia versus Princeton . . . can I what? Hmmm . . . I see . . . well, you tell Mr. Weinroth to call me. Give him my number and I'll see what I can do . . . anything for you, champ . . . I know. I hear her . . . well, keep squeezing that ball . . . A week from Saturday . . . be good now . . . say hello to your sister for me. Yes. Goodby."

He sighs and turns to me. "My son," he explains. "In the eighth grade. Going to be a fine athlete, Mack. Good coordination and good power for a boy his age. One minute, if you'll excuse me. I don't write things down, I never remember. When will I get organized? Ah, Benjamin, Benjamin." He goes to his typewriter and types something, leaves it in the roller. "If I don't leave it here I'll forget. For his club at his Jewish Center, they're having a big breakfast for fathers and sons and he said that I could get some ballplayer to speak to them. In the past, you see, I've been able to get speakers for them — Sid Gordon a few times, Cal Abrams once, "Goody" Rosen. They have another young Jewish boy from Brooklyn on the team this year

— maybe I can get him. If he tames his wildness he will be all right. Like Rex Barney. Remember him?"

He comes back and sits down across from me. "You see, my wife, she can't live with me, I can't live with her — what's the difference? — but every day, she finds some reason to call me. It's crazy, I tell you. I send her money every month —" He shakes his head. "But why should I give you my troubles?" He looks up at me. "You, you have your own, heh? So. At least to my boy I am important — I get tickets to the Garden, the Polo Grounds, Ebbets Field, anywhere — we take his friends along sometimes and I get some of the players to speak with them. It's something. Some- day, though, someday he'll pass me and then what? He'll say, my father's still an adolescent. He spends his life getting conniptions over the newest eighteen year old with a jump shot. Will he be right?" He stops, but I know he don't want me to answer him. "Here," he says, looking down at his sheet. "I have listed a series of questions. You don't bite on one, I progress to another. So. It is now established *why* you did what you did — for the money. That is motive. So next I ask: why did you want the money? Why so much so soon?"

"Oh man, that's easy," I say.

"Yes?"

Then I tell him how when I was young I had this dream. Oh yeah, I had a dream. I sip some beer. I been waiting for this one. I tell him how when I was young my mother got me all these books so I could *be* somebody. Books about Negroes. I read about this

Booker T. Washington and this Carver and his peanuts, but the stories I liked most, they were the ones
about the athletes. Jack Johnson and Satchel Paige
and Jesse Owens and Joe Louis. My old man, Joe
Louis fighting somebody, he glued to the radio. He
talk about him all the time. So I got out stuff on Louis
and put his picture up on my wall with his puffy lips.
Yeah. I shadow box and my old man he cheer me on.
I read how Joe Louis, he was born in Alabama, and
raised in the slums of Detroit and becomes the
youngest guy ever to win the heavyweight title. He's
twenty-three. I got the facts, huh? Yeah. He's the
Brown Bomber and he licks everybody, except Schmel-
ing who he gets back good in the first round. I remember after the war, my old man excited and then
Louis KO'ing Billy Conn. Yeah. And I read in his
life story about how the first thing he did when he
had a lot of money was to buy a big house for his
mother. That's my dream, see. I go to my old man
and I say to him that when I become champ I'm gonna
buy him and my mother a house the way Louis did and
he tells my old lady and they gas to everybody about
what I say. Oh yeah. I'm the golden boy, little Black
Bomber, me. Gonna be a credit to my people, make
something of myself. Then the first time I see Louis
fight it's in a bar with my old man, he's out of retirement and on this small TV tube running away from
Jersey Joe Walcott. He ain't got it no more so I give
up being world heavyweight champ. But Louis, he's
got these evil managers, see. I read about them too.

How he makes millions but somehow everybody takes advantage of him, he don't know what's coming off. Man, I say, that's pretty bad. You got to watch out. My old man, he still asks me about that house I'm gonna buy some day. But houses, you can't buy them playing basketball, so when the opportunity comes knocking I say to myself, Mack baby, now you can pay your parents back for all they done for you. Now you can make them proud. Now you can save up and be a good son the way Joe Louis was. Buy them a big house to live in. Oh yeah, I had a dream, babe. Rosen, he's on the edge of his seat, scribbling away, he real surprised by all I know. I'm high, man. Flying.

"Jack Johnson!" I hear. "How many would know of him? And Louis — that surprises me too. I would think you would be more attracted to Sugar Ray. Louis stalked, Sugar dances!"

"But Louis, man, he had the power."

"Yes," Rosen says, smiling. "But how — how do you know, if you didn't see him in his prime? By the time you saw him he was gone — as you say, he ran away from Walcott. Then in his comeback in '49, Ezzard Charles — a second-rate light-heavy — embarrassed him."

I shrug. "I saw films. And I read."

"Yes, yes. Maybe we remember what we read even more than what we see. So. I remember believing that Dempsey was the world's greatest — better than Johnson or Corbett or Sullivan — long before I ever saw him in the ring. And you know what? When I saw him, it was disappointing. I had expected muscles of steel, coal smeared on his body. Ha! The arguments my friends and I used to have about who was the greatest fighter — Corbett, Sullivan, Fitzsimmons — and others: Burns, Kid McCoy, Levinsky and the great Stanley Ketchel — for hours we could debate. And none of us had ever seen a professional fight — or even a film of one. Listen — did you ever hear of Battling Siki?"

"Who?"

He laughs. "I thought not. I did my first feature story on him. In 1922, when I was writing for the old *New York World,* Siki was light heavyweight champion of the world. He knocked out Georges Carpentier in six rounds in Paris. I remember writing up the action from the teletype, as if I were there. Siki was a Sengalese Negro, you see. I remember that. How could I forget it? It gave, how should I put it, *romance* to my column." It's his turn now, he gasses on. "Carpentier, you know, had already been beaten by Dempsey. Dempsey — did you know he fought until 1940? Knocked out three men in that year, too. But Robinson, he is the best of all. Louis — all right, so he had the power, but not the grace, Mack. If it had not been so sweltering hot for the Joey Maxim fight, Sugar Ray would have been light heavyweight champion also. Then heavyweight. Now that he's back from retirement and champion again, who can tell? Did you see him beat Bobo Olsen in May? Ah —" He comes at me stronger. "I remember something, Mack — I remember. It fits. So! Do you know where I was when the basketball scandals first broke in 1951?" I shrug. "I was watching Sugar Ray in Chicago! Yes. Can you name the fight?"

"What's this — a quiz program?"

Rosen laughs. "No, no. I'll tell you. He was demolishing Jake Lamotta, the Bronx Bull, the man who had defeated poor Marcel Cerdan. It was terrible. In ninety-five fights — until he met Sugar Ray — Lamotta had never been knocked down." He stops. "You," he says. "You reminded me of Sugar Ray on a basketball court." Then he's gone, flying like I was, his fingers curling in the air. "How does one describe him, his straightened hair slapping his forehead, his arms and legs moving like a tap dancer, supple, loose, energetic — the perfect fighter. Yes. I remember even in high school, covering the P.S.A.L. playoffs, how out of place you looked among those driving aggressive New York City boys. You, only you had style, Mack! In college, also. At the Garden. And when I saw your name in the papers, while in Chicago, I made the connection. The quickness of the cat, the power of the lion — you and Sugar Ray." He's breathing hard, voice rising. "And your body. Your body — it was like — like —" Then he stops and looks at me, blinks like. "Walker Smith," he says. "Walker Smith."

"Who?"

He stands up. "That was Sugar Ray's real name. Was? Is — who knows how long he will go on? Just some information for your quiz show. Ha!" He laughs and walks around the room, breathing. "Quiz shows! Do you watch them? They've replaced everything on the airwaves. Everything." He cackles and comes over to me, pats my shoulder. "I have an idea, Mack. Maybe, we put you in an isolation booth next time you come here." He goes away. "Don't get me wrong, now. Everything you've told me I have down. But we must expand our vistas, proceed to other questions. Remember, Mack, you are a symbol of the big-time corruption which corrodes our national fiber!" He's bent over, laughing.

I switch on. That the Rosen I know from the telephone. I remember now. "Hey," I say. "I got a question for you. I mean now — tonight — it's like you're talking all this stuff serious, man. How come? Those columns! Shit. You don't believe them any more than me."

"Your question?"

"What you mean?"

"You said you had a question for me." He cocks his head to one side, grinning.

"Cut the shit, man. The way you were talking just before, with the quiz shows and that symbol stuff — like you said on the phone, we understand each other. But all that other jazz. What you up to?"

He goes back to his papers. "Here," he says. "Statistics. Do you know what percentage of Big Ten football players ever complete their degrees? And here —! In January of 1951, just before the scandals broke, the N.C.A.A. voted, 130 to 60, to abolish its Sanity Code, a Code which specified that paying jobs for athletes

had to be commensurate with work. See? Those foul
lines —"

"Look," I say, getting mad. "Don't bug me, man.
Just tell me what you up to—"

"You ask if I take this affair seriously? Seriously?
Of course I am serious! I told you. I have plans,
Mack. Schemes —"

"Like what?"

"Ah," he says, leaning back. Again. "Ah."

"What, man?"

"Be patient. In time, in time."

I get up and go toward him. "I had enough gas for
one night," I say. "I earned my twenty-five bills."

"Mack," he says, putting his hand on my arm. "You
did earn the money. That's what this is all about.
I'm trying to convince you that you shouldn't feel
guilty. Don't you understand? The money is yours.
You *earned* it."

I shove him down in his chair. He bounces up. He
got that serious look in his eye. Don't like that look.
It the one I remember from way back, the one said:
you be somebody, you make something of yourself.
"You fucken right I earned it," I say.

"But," he says, "if you really believe me, then why
are you so angry about it? Don't you see, Mack?"

"One other thing," I say. Say it all now and be done
with it. "You better leave off trailing me around."

"What?"

"Come off it, man. Don't play dumb. Just stop
following me —"

"But I'm not," he says. "Oh my Mack!" He turns

around, his hand on his forehead. "Why?" he asks, coming back. "See? See what it has come to? Trust me, Mack."

"If you ain't following me, call off whoever is, you hear?"

"But Mack —" He comes at me again and I can't take it. This time I shove him down good. Next thing I know he's flipped his bean, dancing around me, his guard up, throwing jabs. I got to keep spinning to follow him. "Ha!" he says. "Push me down, heh? You didn't know I was once a boxer, did you?" He flicks out a left, open handed. He touch me, I'll murder him. "On the lower east side I learned. In the streets and at the Educational Alliance. Benny Leonard coached me — told me I had the makings. Old Abe Attell too. Ha!" He bobs his head, then does a combination of rights and lefts against the air. "Once I sparred with Corporal Izzy Schwartz, the flyweight champion of the world in 1928. And Abe Goldstein, bantamweight champ, he taught me what to do in the clinches." He's breathing hard, dancing. "You want to spar with me, fellow? Ha! Try to hit me. Come. Try!" He gives a rat-a-tat-tat with his left, moves pretty good for an old man. "Come, hit me. Try. You can't do it, I'll bet. I have the moves, Mack. Watch my head. Left. Right. Come, try to hit me, monster!" Then he makes his mistake. He fakes with two left jabs, crosses with a right, flicks my chin with a left. "Ha! Hit me. Try!" He comes in again, dancing left. I turn around. He hops over a pile of newspapers, comes in low. I wait. "Working on the bag," he says, and runs through a series of circle lefts and rights. He tries to crouch down but his belly won't let him. Then before I know it he lands a good one on my cheek, slap! jumping up to reach me. That's all. I swing out at his face. Miss. "See!" he says. "I told you you couldn't touch me." I wait. He comes in again shuffling to the right now, in front of his easy chair where his pad is. He tosses a left, then a right, then a left hook and I see it coming way off, for my ear. I go to grab it, it's gone and he sneaks a right into my gut. It don't hurt. He cackles and keeps dancing. How he keep it up, I don't know. "Try to hit me. Come try!" Okay, I say. "Try!" But I don't try to slug, I just move straight in on him and lift him off his dancing legs. "See!" he says, his puss almost flush against mine. "See! In your eyes, I see it. You do relish murder! You do want revenge! You *do*, Mack. To get even. I know. I *know!*" I feel my muscles all tense and he's right, man. You know it. "Oh, my breath," he says. "My heart." Then he laughs. "Pretty good for an old timer, heh? I surprised you, did I not?" He's still breathing hard. "Oh my breath," he says. "My right arm, it hurts." He looks worried, then smiles again. "You should not have shoved me, see? I have some tricks left. Oh your eyes, Mack. The murder in them! Why kill me? With my pains, I will die soon enough on my own. Why accrue more guilt?" Don't like his talk, but the murder he talk about, that gone too. I drop him down, but before I quit I grab his fat nose in my fingers and give it a real good twist, feel the bone. Oh man, he howls! Then I laugh some. He falls back into his chair, both hands round his nose. "Oh, oh!" he groans.

"See you, Rosen," I say, head for the door. "Thanks for the scratch, man."

"Mack!" he calls. "Mack!"

"Keep your nose clean, champ," I say, opening the door. "Watch your daughter's ass."

"Mack! Mack!"

Then I move out.

FIVE

I GET OUTSIDE I feel better. Air hits me. I walk down Church Avenue, past the Kenmore Theater. Across the street the old church, used to cut classes and sit in the graveyard. They got famous men buried there, my mother says, Indians too. In front of Garfield's Cafeteria all the guys hanging out with their broads and their puffed hair. I go by, there this one black girl, she got platinum hair teased up like a beehive. Willa see that, she put that babe in her place. Guys with Erasmus jackets on. Where's mine? I keep walking. Past the firehouse and the Holy Cross schoolyard. Too early to go home, they just bug me again about where I been keeping myself. I get home when everybody sleeping, all they got's breakfast to bother me. I think. Maybe I get enough from Louie and Rosen, I move out. Yeah. About time, too. Maybe me and Willa, we set up a place together, get another room. I get on the subway at Nostrand Avenue and head uptown. That Rosen! Man, what's with him? I got to laugh, him boxing. Like the way he swallow my story, though. I keep him going with these interviews, maybe I do okay. This guy comes walking through the subway car, about Franklin Avenue, tapping his cane, making believe he's blind with vaseline shit smeared on his eyes. This guy on a date, he puts some coins in. Maybe I should of been a boxer, my size. But man, you get your ass handed to you, wind up with half a brain. Like the football players at college. They were in the dorm next to ours and they had to bust their asses for their money. Football makes more money than us. Oh yeah. They real valuable property. You think they don't work hard, you wrong, babe. They practicing all spring, all summer, out killing themselves, knocking heads when it's freezing. Crazy, you ask me. You get hurt there, you finished for good. One guy, my freshman year, dumbass don't put his cup in and they tear his balls apart. Guy comes to my room, everybody talking about it, says you never seen such a mess. They sew him up, but who knows what happens to him. Guys in that dorm always walking around with casts and slings and stuff. Man, everytime I think of that guy I get the chills, picture his pretty pink ball hanging loose, dripping blood — Jesus, what's with you, Mack? What you thinking of things like that? After Louis, only fighter I really liked, that Gene Hairston, nickname him Gene "Silent" Hairston cause he was born deaf. He's a pretty good fighter. I remember him. Only Kid Gavilan with his bolo punches, he knocks crap out of him. Wonder what it's like to get hit and not hear it. Thinking about that guy on the football team reminds me of when I was scared they gonna draft me, ship my ass off to fight chinks in Korea. In the schoolyard, the guys say that in the war, the Japs, they used to line you up, your hands behind your back and dance these naked women in front of you. You ain't got no clothes on and when your dick goes up, they come along with these big curved swords and chop it off. Sweat coming up through my pants, remembering. I don't feel too good. Maybe it's that sandwich Rosen give me.

I get out of the subway at 72nd Street. Need that air. All the fags hanging around the park there. How come so many spics make it this way? I walk up Broadway, trying to forget Louie and Rosen, then let myself into Willa's. The place empty and I sack out for a while, till this knocking on the door wake me. Mrs. Fontanez got Willie in her arms, says she saw me come in, would I mind watching Willie so she can get to sleep. Three of her kids behind her, hanging on to her skirt, sucking thumbs. I take Willie and she smile at me. Says she's glad I'm Willa's friend, if I want my palm read sometime she do it for free. Oh yeah, that's all I need. I got a future, me. I take him into the room and he starts wailing, first thing. I shove his bottle into his mouth, dumb Willie, he wrap his fat lips around that nipple, that all he need. Getting to be a regular father, me. I open the refrigerator, there a big chocolate cake there, white icing say 4 MACK on it. Willa, she's crazy! I take a chunk out of it with some milk and lean back on the couch, looking through a magazine about how to fix up your house, then the phone rings. "Yeah?" I say.

"Ah," Rosen says. "I thought I would find you there. So. How are you?"

"How *am* I?" I got to laugh. "Rosen — one thing I got to admit, you got balls."

"What else?" He cackles. "But this I know. I have

something you want, otherwise you'd have already shaken me. See — you don't hang up." He waits. "All right, maybe there is something you can give to me also. But I say this: let us be more honest. Now, that story you told me about Joe Louis, Mack — who would believe such nonsense? Do you think you had me fooled?"

"You believe what you want."

"All right, all right." Willie turn over on his stomach, crack his head against the side of the bed. Don't hurt it, though. Must be rock. "I hear you sighing," he says. "So. I will get to the point. I have one question for you: would you like to play professional basketball, to be reinstated?"

"C'mon, man!" I say.

"Do not be angry. I am serious — I have never been more serious. There are ways, Mack. Ways. Have you ever heard of anti-trust proceedings?"

"Maybe."

"All right. Here. Let me tell you something of what I have in mind: a brief outline. In 1951 when you shaved points, you did not come under the D. A.'s power the way the boys from City did because you played in Ohio, and at that time Ohio had no sports bribery statute. So. Society says you are not a criminal. What are you then? A basketball player. How can you ply your trade? You cannot — because the N.B.A. says you cannot. But — and here's the rub — they are involved in interstate commerce; therefore this is conspiracy — and to conspire to keep you from playing is illegal. There! My argument. What do you think?"

"You think with your nose, Rosen."

"Mack. Please. Don't you see? You and the boys like yourself, all doors are closed to you. Like Jews, heh? No place to go. You are able, qualified, free of sin — but the league has put the mark of Cain on you. Enough. Business. There are legal matters to be worked out — my theory must be checked out with a lawyer. But before I go ahead I need a commitment from you, Mack. With your background, your clean record, your color — ha! let's face it, why not use it?— I think we can have a case."

"What you get out of it, man?"

"Ah," he says. "A certain pleasure, let us say. The high and the mighty, the righteous — those who are as guilty as you — they crumble. Money? All right, I'll take a little. A slice from the lawyer's cut. So. Are you with me?"

"I'll let you know."

"Fine, Mack. Fine. I ask no more. In the meantime, perhaps you should begin working out again in the schoolyard, or in some gym. Get ready. This may take time, but if you are willing, I —"

"I said I'll let you know."

"Thank you, Mack," he says. "God bless you. We can be a good team, you and me. We can do things! Oh — one last thing. My nose. It's all right, so don't worry." Then he hangs up. Crazy guy. Who he kidding with this scheme of his, but what I got to lose?

Like he say, it be a long time before we even get to court. You ask me, we never get there and during that never, I take in a lot of scratch for doing nothing but letting him get hot over his ideas. I take a nap, Willa comes home, we have some fun then I talk to her, tell her about what's been happening, Louie and Rosen. I tell her about *Louie's Leapers,* she gets excited.

"Can I play?" That's all she wants to know. I tell her it's a tough league, she says she's tough too. I tell her what if it's men only written in the rules somewhere. She says she'll shave her hair. "Hell," she says, "mostly white boys playing and looking, they won't know the difference."

"Yeah," I say. "But what you gonna do with your tits?"

"Oh man, I just strap 'em down, and wear a droopy sweatshirt. No kidding, Mack. How bout it?" She grabs me around the neck, nuzzles me. "Mmm, boy, that be the end, you and me making it together on the court! What's the matter, you afraid I'm too good for you? Don't worry, I'm not a gunner. I'll pass off to you, so you can be the star. Sure. You be the star while we go far! How's that? Remember, I got a mean hook shot, babe. I'm mean and you're lean. Mean and lean, us. How'd you like my cake, huh? Nothing like devil's food cake to build strong athletes!" She squeezes my arm-muscle, rests her head on my chest. "Oh Mack, you're so strong!" Then she's laughing, jumping over me, onto the floor, to the refrigerator. She comes back, a glass of milk in her hand and the plate with the rest of the cake. "Want some?" she

asks. "It's real good. One thing you got to admit,
I can cook." She drinks the whole glass without stopping, then wipes the white off her mouth. "Man, how
we work up an appetite! C'mon — you want the last
piece of this cake? Bet you're hungry too. Admit it.
You're hungry, too. Right?"

"Okay," I say and when she reaches over and feeds
me the piece of that cake, me not using my own hands,
the crazy look, it goes out of her eyes for a minute
and inside me, first time all day, the thing been holding all my muscles tight against each other, it lets
everything loose, specially round my face, like they
took some iron mask off it, and when she smiles at
me with her gold tooth, shit! Only thing bothers me,
is my stomach feels like it don't want to hold the cake
somehow, not like I got to throw up, just like under
the breast bone, acids or something let loose too. I
guess I smile back, cause she puts the back of her
hand next my face and I put my hand there and press
it to my cheek. It's warm. "Listen, Willa — " I say,
but the minute I speak, that nice feeling get confused.
"Don't say it, huh?" she says, puts the plate with
chocolate crumbs down on the floor. "What for? Just
one thing I got to ask you — me and Willie, we ain't
supporting the country. How long you gonna live off
us like this? We don't mind, now. You know that,
right? You know it. But you stay here, buddy, you
fork over some cash. Okay? Make with the money,
honey. That's all we ask."

"Sure," I say.

She gets up, puts her robe on. "Sure how much?"

she asks. "Not everywhere you get a cook like me thrown in. Tell you what, though, you let me play on your team, I make an adjustment after a while. Okay?"

I get up and put my pants on, get my wallet out and take out a ten. One of Rosen's. "Here," I say. "For tonight."

"Oh, come on, man, huh?" she says, hands wide on her hips. "Why you got to be like that? You a grow-ing boy, like Willie, and you got a big appetite is all. Why you so angry, babes?"

"Who's angry? You asked for cash, here it is. Now we got an agreement."

She puts her hand to her head. "Oh man, you is so *out* of it! Who brung you up is what I want to know. You know what you are sometimes? You a big baby, a big momma's baby is what you are. Man, every-body gotta be so careful what they say and do to you. Who you think you are? — Look, all I asked is that you chip in for a little grub, is all." She comes over and touches my hair, gentle. "Don't take me the wrong way, huh, Mack? Oh Mack, my Mack. What we gonna do with you? Here," she says, picking the ten spot off the table. "Take it back. I can manage. You want the truth, I thought *you'd* feel better, you help out. Ah, what's the difference? How you feel, babe? Better?" She gets in back of me, arms hugging me around my neck. Why I fight so much? I rest my cheek against her forearm, she sees I'm loose. "That's all!" she says, breaks away. "Kiss your ten bucks good-bye," and she puts it in this tin can on top of the refrigerator. Then she's back, driving and pulling me to the bed. "So?" she keeps asking. "What you gonna do now, huh babes? Come on. Answer up. Quick!"

"What I gonna do about what?"

"You know, babes. About me playing on your team. Honest, Mack honey. If I strap 'em down and put on a big sweat shirt, we could have fun! Come on, let me play, huh?"

"I got to think it over," I say.

Okay. I explain to Willa, it's not the money, but I remember something, got to take off. On the subway, 42nd Street, these three kids get on, one of them starts pounding away on these bongo drums, this little kid, he can't be more than five-six the most, he starts jitterbugging down the subway car, the third guy, he the biggest, he claps his hands, it wakes people up. This little kid, he's okay. He keeps his balance good, I figure him for a halfback some day. He grabs onto the poles in the middle of the car, twirls himself upside down, you get scared he gonna fall and break his head, then he comes flying down the aisle, cartwheeling, splits his legs wide open, heads the other direction, keeps jitterbugging and splitting till we get to 34th Street. We start to pull in, the big guy goes quick down the aisle with a baseball cap, people throwing in money. They come to me, I take out a five dollar bill, don't ask me why, say I want to talk with them. The big guy, he's the boss, he says for five bucks they stop putting on their show till 14th Street.

"You make good money?" I ask.

"We do okay," the boss says. He's real cool. Oh

yeah. You gonna learn a lot from him. The little kid, did all the dancing, he got no expression in his eyes. They explain to me, how when he gets old enough, he works his way up, first bongos, then collecting. The boss, he says he used to do the dancing, but he's on top now, too old to dance. The little kid tells me he got his little brother in training, take over for him soon. The bongo player, looks part spic, he just leans forward chewing gum, looks like he's on dujie. Oh yeah. These kids making it. Someday they all be strung out good. Maybe I get Ronnie, go into business with them. We call ourselves the Subway Five. Oh yeah. Ronnie, he be bopping away one end of the car with his bass, the others doing their stuff, I go around collect the money, who gonna say no to me? My size, it count for a lot then. 14th Street, they go into their act again, I figure, we get Willa on our team too, Ed Sullivan he be booking us once a month, before we get through, we own the subways. What gets me is how the little kid, he does somersaults and splits in a moving train, one end to the other, his face don't change. Dull brown, man. He flips over once, not using his hands, this old lady with shopping bags about has a heart attack. They collect again, the boss comes up to me like everybody else, I don't put nothing in this time. I tell him not to suck blood, he just goes onto the next guy.

"Hey, lemme talk to you, son," I say to the little kid, he looks at his boss, his boss shrugs, he comes to me.

"You makin' good money?" I say.

He don't answer. His sneakers, they like Adlai's, got holes on the bottom. I ask him some more questions, but he don't got no tongue now, don't seem too interested in me. Train's getting on toward Brooklyn, his boss figures they got to work uptown, he calls the little kid. I tell him there's no future in this dancing stuff, he letting the big kid use him.

The big kid hears me, looks at me dirty, but it don't make no difference. He just grabs the little kid by his sweater, yanks him off the train. I get up quick but the doors close. The big kid stands on the other side, don't look scared. "Just leave off my property, big man," he says through the window. The train moves out, so I sit down, sleep the rest of the way, get into my room quiet. I put the desk light on, sit on the edge of Ronnie's bed for a while, watching him make these wet sounds with his mouth. I shake him and he sits up, rubs his eyes.

"Hey, Mack! How you doing?"

"Okay."

"How come you're home?" He sits up some more. "Boy, you should hear the old lady go on about you, you gone all the time now."

"Save it," I say. "I got something to talk to you about."

"Sure. What's up?"

"Listen," I say. "We got to get warmed up. I mean, you got your sneakers here, how about us going to the schoolyard tomorrow morning?"

He about hugs me. "Do you mean it?" he says.

"Yes or no," I say. "You got school?"

"Ah, what's the difference? Sure I'll come."

He wants to talk more but I cut him off. "Okay," I say, standing up and undressing, getting ready to sleep. "At breakfast we'll make like we going out same as always. You take the basketball, say it's for after school." He's leaning on his elbow, resting his head. "I can still show you something. There's a lot of things you can do with a basketball." I put out the light. In the morning we do like we planned, get over to Holy Cross schoolyard and shoot around a while, work on his jump shot. He's got a good touch, but he be better he lets that ball go from over his shoulder instead of from his chest. You get blocked too much that way. It's pretty cold out, our breath steaming the air, but who cares? I'm feeling good, man, coaching Ronnie, playing him one-on-one, hearing that ball crash into the backboard, drop through. Only thing is, we there about an hour, maybe less, these kids start coming into the yard in their Catholic uniforms and all these cats in their black capes telling them what to do. They chase us off, tell us they gonna call the cops we don't leave. Man, what they want? We go into the candy store at Bedford Avenue, have some coffee, talk some, Ronnie wanting to know all he done wrong, when we gonna do this again. I tell him I take off from work Saturday, we come back. He says he got band practice, but he'll come down after.

By the time I get down there Saturday it's one o'clock, pretty nice weather, there's guys sitting around

all along the fence, smoking and talking. With Louie's
and Willa and stuff I ain't been down here a long time,
I get a big hello from the guys. Oh yeah. I'm a hero
here too. "Hey, Mack babe — how's it going?" this
guy, Yuddie Rudy, played backcourt for Erasmus
with me says. "Say there, Plastic Man, how you feel?
You want next with me?" this other guy says. Sure,
I say, sit next to him, I see the young kids, their eyes
all looking me up and down like I was Duke Snider
or somebody. "Me, Yuddie and you," this guy says,
then starts gassing with me like I known him forever.
I don't mind, though. I just lean back, my arms along
the fence, listen to him, watch the game going on,
talk to guys about what they been doing, where
they working. Some big boys on the court, none of
them as big as me but big enough. It's rough, man.
You hear bodies. There this one kid I never see before, he's shooting the eyes out of the basket, nobody
gonna stop him, guy next to me says he's from North
Carolina, gonna play for them in a year or two, only
he don't got the grades so he's at this military prep
school now. He stops gassing I feel the sun on me,
nice, look around at all the guys, I swear to God, I feel
like stretching my arms along the fence, making my
right arm turn at the corner, grab them all into me.
The game on the court's over, I go out and warm up,
leave my jacket on. Nobody my size to guard me, so
I tell Yuddie I gonna play outside with him, let this
other cat stay under the boards. This North Carolina
guy, he's about six-two or three, he guards me, first

time I go up for a jumper, he's way up too, gets a
piece of the ball, makes me look bad, the ball don't
even hit the rim. Then he gets it, puts in a long set,
two-handed, next thing you know they got us down
5–1. Yuddie comes over to me, asks if I'm okay, says
I look like I'm in a daze or something. He asks if
I wanna switch men, I tell him no, I'm okay. He's
right, though. I got to wake up. I ain't getting paid
to lose, this game. Trouble is, I'm thinking too much,
thinking about what the guys gonna say about me,
I don't show 'em something. I don't shape up, Louie
too, he gonna forget about giving me some extra long
green and Rosen, he's gonna say Goodby Charlie and
then I gonna come down here, everybody gonna say
hello to me, treat me real nice, all they gonna want
me to do, though, is stay under the boards, get rebounds for them. Won't need legs then. Oh yeah.
Why I can't keep my mind on the game? I look across
the street where they tearing up this building, used to
be a Democratic Club where my old man went a few
times to get out of jury duty, I see Ronnie huffing
down the street, lugging his bass over his shoulder.
He starts across, a car almost hits him. "Cut, Mack!"
I hear Yuddie say, I shift left, break right and that
pass comes at me face high, nice, I start like I'm
gonna follow with a hook shot right, before North
Carolina knows it I'm scooping that ball up the other
way spinning it off the backboard, the guys along the
fence, they know they seeing Mack play ball! "Okay,"
I say. We take it out again, they get it to me, all I
got to do is take two steps, stop real short and North

Carolina keeps going like I'm gonna take that third step, I'm up in the air all alone, suspended there, man, that ball resting nice and light in my hand I wing it for the hoop like there's a magnet there drawing it soft and easy and we only down by two. Next time I head for a drive, see Yuddie moving behind me, I go up for the shot, got three men hanging on my arms but that ball, Yuddie's got it under the basket for an easy layup, the guys by the fence whistle. I can pass, too, babes. "How long I gotta wait for next?" I hear my brother say, he comes walking in. I watch him, he sits down by the fence, takes his shoes off, starts to lace up his sneakers. He trying real hard not to look at me. This other guy on our team, he puts in a lucky drive, the score's tied, then I go to work, man, ain't nobody gonna stop me now. North Carolina, he got hands, he bumps me I move through, but it don't matter, I'm flying over him, don't even see the guys along the side now, just love that ball, the way it bounces off the concrete, feel sweat dripping down inside my shirt. North Carolina gets the ball once, starts to his right, thinks he has me fooled, when he goes up for the jumper I'm up there too, a foot over his head I bang that ball down, stuff him so hard when that ball comes to him next time he passes off quick. Oh yeah. He ain't so tough. I tell Yuddie let's end the game, I go into the pivot the first time, yell over to Ronnie to watch. North Carolina boxing me out, got his elbow in my back. Yuddie shoots a long one-hander but it don't go in, he shoots it too hard like it's gonna go right over the rim, only the ball and me, we got a date, man, I'm up there just before the rim, grab it with both hands and lead that ball where it wants to go, plunge it through over my head you hear the guys whistle and cheer for that. I pat North Carolina on the ass, tell him he played a good game. Yuddie yells "Next — " and I wink at Ronnie.

After a while I tell the guys I'm not as young as I was, I gotta rest some, need something to drink. These little kids, they hang around the fence you give 'em money they get you sodas. They do okay, they hang around all day, keep the deposits. When it comes Ronnie's turn for next I say okay, I play one more game, tell him to work the play me and Yuddie did before. He throws the ball too hard first two times, third time, though, we make it. I try setting him up most of the game, he's real nervous at first. You can tell. Along the side, guys all teasing him about having his big brother to protect him, but who cares? He gets the touch after a while, puts in four out of five shots clean and we win easy. I give somebody else my game, say I got to take off, I wave goodby everybody tells me to take it easy, Mack, keep my arms loose, be good. Oh yeah. I'm gonna be real good, me. The Penguin, he gonna have lots more clippings for his scrapbook, my rate. The Penguin, he just call me once since that time, tells me to keep my dirty hands off his wife. I tell him he means my black hands but he says he means my dirty hands, that he's warning me. The Penguin, you got to hand it to him, he got something to say to me, he says it. I figure I'm doing okay now with the loot coming in from Rosen and Louie, I stop by his place, get me a new pair of slacks or something.

I head up Flatbush Avenue, feel the sweat drying on me inside, that's a nice feeling, get to his store, you never seen a guy so glad to see you. He got this yellow tape measure round his neck, he about wears my hand out shaking it. "How's it been, Mack babe?" he says. "Sure am glad to see you. How's it going? Hey Pop — say hello to Mack here! You remember Mack, don't you?" His old man, looks just like him, only bald, he comes over to me, says hello, asks me what I'm doing. "Making it, man," I say and the Penguin laughs, pats his old man on the back and sends him away, takes me into a corner with overcoats. "About what happened with Bev, what I said — " he starts. "I know what she — "

"Forget it," I say.

"Where you been?" he asks.

"Holy Cross."

"You mean it? Boy, I wish I didn't have to work on Saturdays," he says. "I'd give anything to be able to spend a day over there — " Then he's asking me to name off all the guys who were there and what they're doing and things. I'm feeling so good, almost tell him about Rosen's plan, how maybe I'm gonna be playing in the pros soon, but the minute I think of that, I get mad. Who I fooling? You got to watch out, Mack babe, I say, else Rosen, he gonna get you thinking crazy like him. Stay cool, man. The Penguin, he's taking me over to these racks got jackets and suits on them, tells me to pick out what I want,

he'll give it to me at a good price. I say okay, pick
out this nice tweed, brown with some green in it, reminds me of a jacket Big Ed used to have, the Penguin measures me, puts these chalk marks all over,
says he'll have the tailor let the sleeves out. I ask
him how much, he says forget it. "I ain't a charity
case, man," I say. He says he's sorry, he didn't mean
to offend me, tells me the jacket cost him seventeen
bills. I tell him he's full of it, he says it's the truth,
then he tells his old man to watch the store and we
go over to Church Avenue, grab a pizza in *Luigi's*.
We used to go there every Friday night, after games
at Erasmus and the Penguin starts in talking like he
does about all the things we done together in high
school and college, tells me I was nuts sometimes.
There was this one ref, see, used to be on my back
all the time, worked a lot of our games, so finally, he
calls charging on me, I tell him I gonna get him some
night after a game in a dark alley, gonna kill him.
The Penguin he was with me, we get that ref after
the game in the parking lot, the Penguin, he pushes
him back against a car with his umbrella, talks like
Peter Lorre. He's real good at imitating him, says
"Mack would like to talk with you. He has something
very important to say — " Then I whip out this gun,
my face as mad as can be and tell him I told him I
was gonna kill him, the Penguin asks him if he got
any last words and then I pull that trigger, you hear
the shots bounce all over the parking lot, that ref,
man, he probably leaked in his pants, those blanks
went off. The Penguin, he got the gun from this friend

of his who acted in plays. We leave, the Penguin says to stop by soon, get my jacket, it'll be ready Tuesday. "Stay cool, Penguin," I say. "See you, Plastic Man," he says and we both laugh, head in different directions on Church Avenue. Willa, she gonna like the jacket.

PART TWO

SIX

"So," ROSEN SAYS to me. "When is the big game?"
"You tell me," I say.

"All right," he says, going over to his desk. Still
don't have that mess organized. "Here. So I shouldn't
forget to be there. Wednesday night at 8 o'clock
at Congregation Shaare Torah Gymnasium, *Louie's
Leapers* versus the *Brownsville Bombers*. See — I
have my ticket already. Basketball game for the B'nai
B'rith Championship. Donation: One Dollar. Perhaps you will win a trophy. What do you think,
Mack?"

Then he cackles the way he does. Oh yeah. I'm
back in the bigtime. Me and *Louie's Leapers*, we
burning up our league, win seventeen games in a
row. These last few months, between games and
Willa and these sessions with Rosen, you want to
keep up with me, you got to run, man. Got to work
too, go home sometimes, go to the schoolyard with
Ronnie to coach him when we're free. Oh yeah.
Ronnie, he does okay too. Makes his high school team
easy so I go to his games too. We talk after about
what he's doing right and wrong.

"You know what?" Rosen says, sitting himself down
across from me. "I find that I am looking forward to
seeing you play again. Do you know who is on the
opposing team? The great Nat Morgan! Ah, poor boy,

he too was deprived of his livelihood. He was not as fortunate as you, however. He bribed other boys to do what he did and so he went to the penitentiary." He stops. "Well. I wonder what Morgan is doing now, how he earns his keep. They say he is mixed up in bad things — is that so?" I keep my mouth shut. Morgan, he was born dumb, he gonna die the same way. But Rosen's right about one thing, that mother can play ball. He's on a court, you got yourself a game. He'd be in the pros, he'd be the best. I admit that.

"Here," Rosen says, handing me a sheet of paper. "Perhaps this will get a rise out of you. I've been saving it, to be used at the proper time. What do you think?" He stands in back of me, his finger tips touching my shoulder. "I thought I would put it at the bottom of my column tomorrow or the next day, in my *Rosen's Rumors* section — "

ROSEN'S RUMORS: Word is afoot that the N.B.A. is about to have its hands full with an anti-trust suit, the biggest in sports history! It seems some of the players involved in the 1951 betting scandals are ready to go to court. They say the mistake the N.B.A. made is the old one of the blacklist. You can't do that, boys!

"I'm on a blacklist, huh?" I say. I got to laugh. "That's pretty good. What list they got for the white boys?" Rosen, he laughs too. "Oh yeah," I say. "You going pretty far, you put a black sheep like me on a black list."

"Good, Mack. Good." Rosen laughs, his eyes shine at me, he leans forward. "And do you know what we will be to professional sports when we get through? We will be the Black Plague, Mack! The Black Plague and the black hand!" Then he starts in again on all this legal stuff, asks me if I know what this double jeopardy is. "Double jeopardy says you cannot try a man twice for the same crime," he says. "Fred Johnson, in attacking baseball's empire, he showed that they were a government within a government. A government within a government! The law will never tolerate that. Morgan received his due from society; the N.B.A. cannot punish him again." He's over me now, breathing fire. "They are a business! Landis, he knew it long ago. After the Federal League, why do you think he made all the players free agents?" He pushes his finger at me. "Because he knew that if any of them contested what the majors had done — every player in baseball would have been made a free agent!" Then he starts gassing about the Mexican League and Danny Gardella and this guy named Chase and this Carnegie Report and I turn him off for a while, think about the game. He gets finished, he falls into his chair. "Stories," he says, "I have stories for you, Mack. But someday, unless you and I stand them on their heads, some day the stories will be gone. The only thing athletes will do is to keep clean, advertise shirts and open bowling alleys when they retire. Power, Mack. You have to get back the power — don't you see?"

"Louis," I say. "He had the power, man."

"That's not what I mean. No! Oh, Mack!" he says, looking down. Then he looks up quick, smiling. "You!" he says, laughing, waving a hand. "Don't forget about my boxing days." He's about to get up from his chair, but I stand up first, push him down. "You got anything else we got to talk about tonight?" I say. "I got things to do."

"All right," he says. "One thing. You still haven't promised that you will go along with me a hundred percent in this, through the courts. Will you?"

"I said I'll let you know."

"When, Mack?"

"Maybe after the game next week."

"And then next week you will put me off again. I know you already."

"Look — I said I'll let you know next week and I will."

He stands up and grabs my hand, happy. "I ask no more," he says. He goes to his desk again, comes back with my envelope. "Open it. Make sure."

"I trust you," I say.

"I know," he says, getting me my coat. "I won't keep you any longer. It's good to have you here, Mack. To talk to you. I'll tell you something else," he says, walking me to the door, holding onto my arm. "There is something about you I believe in, you know. I feel I can — how shall I put it? — I can *depend* on you. So long as I can do something for you, I know you will go along with me. When I am no longer of use — pouf! into the ashcan with me." He opens the door and pushes me. "Go. In another minute my wife will be calling. There is no need for you to sit through that again. Go, Mack." He closes the door behind me and I walk to the elevator. "Mack!" he calls after me, down the hall. "The envelopes are here. Always. Come back soon. Oh — another thing. Be smart. Don't fix next week's game. Remember, New York is not Ohio. There are laws here!" Then he starts laughing again, crazy. I get home, I take the twenty-five he gives me and give it to my mother. "For room and board," I say.

She takes the envelope and puts it down on the kitchen table, not looking at it. She points a finger at me. "Something funny going on, Mack. How come, now that you sleep here now and then — like a boarder — how come now you begin paying for your keep?"

"You don't got to take it," I say. "I just thought — "

She stands up and throws her arms around me, pinning mine to my side. "Oh Mack, you're a good boy! Not take the money? Your mother may be getting old, but she not getting dumb." She kisses me on the cheek, then picks up the envelope, rips it open, goes to her little black book, writes it down, then grabs my hand, pulls me into the living room where my old man is sitting, rocking to his TV program, Ernie Kovacs making him laugh. "Selma! Ronnie!" she calls out and we got a regular family conference going, everybody saying what a nice guy I am to be helping out with the household expenses. Oh yeah, I'm gonna be number one son again. I stay in this

Minit-wash business long enough, I get clean. I get so clean I turn into a white sheep someday. Sure. Then Rosen, he gets me off this blacklist and I be home free. "Hey, Selma," I say. "I got a question for you." My mother sits down on the couch next to Ronnie. "What your organization doing about these black lists?" "Black what?" she asks. "Black lists," I say. "Ain't that discrimination to have black lists? See — I found out that back in '51 when I did what I did, they put me on this black list, so what I want to know is, how you and your legal folks, how you gonna get me off?" "Oh Mack!" she says. "Stop teasing." Then she smiles at me so pretty, I got to put my arm around her. Ronnie, he's just sitting back, his long arms spread across the top of the couch. "A lot of the guys on the team," he says, "their folks come to our games sometimes. Maybe you and Dad — you too, Selma — maybe you can all come see me play some Friday night. If you'd like, I mean." Then we all making plans to go out to eat together a week from Friday night and Ronnie's telling them about how I been teaching him and everything. Oh yeah. I gonna be coach-of-the-year, too. You want the truth, he don't need much coaching. He never be All-American, but he's a good little ballplayer. You just got to tell him something once. Selma, she gets quiet while everybody talking basketball, then she ask when I'm bringing my girl home. "What girl?" I say. She comes to me, touches my arm. "You know," she says. My old man puts his hand over his mouth and giggles. I look at Ronnie. He and Willa, they get along great — we do things together sometimes now — but I give him a look and he knows enough to keep shut. Selma, she keeps after me in front of everybody, asking all about my girl and what's the mystery and when I'm gonna be walking down the aisle and raising kids. What she want is what I want to know. She crazy the way she go on. My mother, she must think it's wacky too cause she shuts Selma up. "You leave Mack alone," she says. "When he's ready to bring his girl home, he'll bring her home. It's not time yet."

"I'm sorry," Selma says. "I was just interested, that's all."

"That's all right," my mother says. "But how come you so interested in whether Mack's getting married? Maybe it's you we gotta be asking questions —" Selma, her eyes open up. "C'mon, Selma — you got some news for us? You got a beau?" Selma smiles, nice. "Maybe," she says. I'm sitting down now and she sits next to me, takes my hand. "The truth, Mack," she says. "I was just teasing you. I didn't mean to get you upset. Really."

"If you want to go get married," I say. "that's okay with me. You got my blessing." Everybody laughs when I say this and Selma tells us to stop. "That Mack," my old man says, "he can put you in your place." You better believe it, I think, cause someday you gonna get yours too. Everybody laughing and happy, how come I'm remembering what my old man said? When I first come home from the university, he howling, rocking in his goddamned rocking chair, drinking and laughing. "You think you almost white, but you turn out to be just another nigger," he says. "You ain't no star no more, Mack. You just an ord'nary nigger." Banging his good hand on the arm of his rocking chair. "See — if you're white you all right, if you brown, stick around, but if you black, get on back!" Banging away. Oh yeah. He had his fun. "And you sure are black, Mack. See — ! If you black, you got to get on back!" My mother didn't pull me away, would of killed him then. But I don't got to pay that no mind, I tell myself. I'm riding a hot streak now — things going good all around. Everything I shoot going in. I got no kicks. Louie, he's giving me ten more a week plus ten bucks a game. Between him and Rosen I do okay. The phone rings, I figure it's the Penguin, but it's for my mother, I hear her talking about me giving in money for the family. At the games sometimes now I think about the Penguin, the way it was, but I got Ronnie playing with me now. He's not supposed to — could get kicked off his high school team if they found out, but he uses a phony name, Sam Clemens. First game, I call him Ronnie a couple times, but after that I get used to calling him Sam. Summers when I was at college I used to play up in the Catskill mountains. All the ballplayers did it, using phony names. Colleges said we could get banned for doing it, but even the coaches used to roam around the hotels watching us. Some of the guys had jobs at the hotels, bellhopping and things, but I just used to drive up weekends with the Penguin. He'd be after snatch. "Jewish snatch," he used to say, "it smells the best of all." Then he'd start sniffing. "Can't you smell it yet, Mack?" he used to say to me riding up in his car. Sniff, sniff. I used to get fifteen or twenty a game, for expenses they called it. Played two games on a weekend, sometimes Wednesday night too, I did okay. Good ballplayers up there. The best. All of them making expense money — guys playing in the pros now, all using phony names like me, lots of them getting lots more than that expense money. Oh yeah. What you think? I wanted to name names of guys, there's nobody would get away free. That goes for the fixes too. You think the guys who got caught were the only guys who dumped, you pretty dumb, man. Before Big Ed ever made me a deal, up there in the mountains guys were talking after games about who was making money. Gamblers, they haunted those games. You be surprised if I name the guys I seen talking with gamblers before games. Oh yeah. I tell you something else. There's guys playing in the pros now, they were betting on point scores back then. Used to play outdoors, under the lights, with all these Jews watching us, dressed up in their shiny clothes. Then after we'd get a place to sleep over and our meals. Sam Spade, that was me. Pretty good, huh? The guys, they used to have fun making up names to go under. Bet you didn't know I played with guys like Winston Churchill and John Garfield and Lamont Cranston. Red Auerbach, coach of the Celtics, he always used to be at one of these hotels and he once came over to me after a game where I kept stuffing this guy had a hotshot college reputation, he said, "You're a good ballplayer, son." Yeah. He asked me what college I was going to. How you think these coaches find out about

ballplayers? Those games — with five or six top ballplayers on each team — they as good as your all-star
games. Better, cause outside, playing on concrete,
using some crazy name, you were real loose, like in
the schoolyard. These guys who went to Catholic colleges, they were in deep, man, wonder who got them
off the hook with the D. A.? Must of been a real
powerhouse. Yeah. I look in the papers once, I see
some guy I played with there, got hands about as
clean as mine, he's coaching pro ball now. I'll tell
you the truth, it's good to be playing on a team
again. We're not bad either, me playing pivot, Ronnie
and Johnson in the corners. Johnson, he's our hatchet
man. Don't mess with him, babes. Smokey, when
he's sober, he plays backcourt with Jim Wilson. Wilson, he's got eyes on all sides of his head. He's still
a young guy, playing with us, he's thinking of fin-
ishing up high school, maybe getting a scholarship
somewhere. It's good playing with a team — makes
time at work go faster too, talking about games
that was and ones that gonna be. My old man got
the TV turned up again and we all sitting around
together watching this Murrow guy barge into some
senator's house. Floyd Patterson, he knocked out
old Archie Moore, so Murrow's gonna visit him too.
Selma digs a nail into the back of my hand. "I've
been talking to you," she says. "Haven't you been
listening?"

"To what?"

"That's what I thought," she says. "Do you want to

watch this?" I shrug. "I have something to talk to you about. Come — "

I get up and we go into her room. She closes the door and I sit down on her bed. She takes a cigarette out, taps it a few times, then lights it. Her room's real nice, with these diplomas and things framed on the walls and lots of stuffed animals all over, like you win at Coney Island. In high school we used to go down and clean the guy out who had the basketball shooting thing. Give the animals out on the subways to girls. The Penguin, he'd sell 'em. The basket was about a foot higher than regulation but once you got the range you couldn't miss.

"I'm sorry about before," she says. "I don't know what got into me. Do you forgive me?"

"Forget it," I say. "What you got on your mind?"

"All right," she says, deciding. She sits down next to me. "I don't know why, but I just feel like telling you. What everybody was teasing me about before — it's the truth. There's this boy at school, and — oh, you know!"

"Know what?"

She laughs and leans against me. "Stop," she says. "It's nice with us, Mack. And — and I just had to tell you. Do you mind?"

"Nah."

"You'll like him. He's — oh, I shouldn't say that. You won't feel free with him now — you'll think you *have* to like him."

"He gonna be my brother?"

She sits up and takes her cigarette from the ashtray on the floor. "We haven't really talked about that yet. I mean, we talk about things like marriage and how many children we want — you know — but he hasn't asked me or anything. We both still have another year of school. He's very kind, Mack. He reminds me of you sometimes — I can talk to him the way we used to talk. Do you remember? Like on Saturday afternoons when we used to go to Prospect Park — rowing or ice-skating — and we'd just talk for hours and hours!" She laughs. "Remember how we would sit here at night sometimes, like this, and talk?"

"What we talk about?" I ask.

"Just things," she says. "I guess I did most of the talking — like now — about whatever was on my mind, school, friends, I don't know. I used to model my new clothes for you, remember?" My old man yells from the living room that they're finished with the senator. I stand up. "The only thing is," Selma says. "I'm afraid to bring him home — I mean, I want to, but I don't want to —"

"What's the matter — you ashamed of us?"

"I deserve that, I suppose," she says. "I don't know why — maybe it's daddy, and the way he acts, or —"

"Hey look," I say. "This guy white?"

She laughs easy. "You don't have to worry about that." She looks straight at me. "Mack?"

"Yeah?"

"This girl — is she?"

"What girl?"

"Oh stop it," she says. "Why won't you *talk* about anything anymore?"

"What's there to talk about?"

"I don't know," she says. "Just — just *things!* I've been telling — no, I won't use that. You don't owe me anything. I didn't tell you my secret so that you should tell me yours. God! I hope I didn't. I like to think I've outgrown that. I'll put it this way — " She licks her lips. " — if you do have a girl, Mack, I'd like to meet her. Just as I'd like you to meet Roy. Okay?"

Ronnie peeks his head into the room. "Hey, come on — Patterson's coming on."

Selma grabs my hand when I start to go. "Well?" she says.

"Well what?"

"Please, Mack — must you be this way?"

"What way?"

"Forget it."

"Tell you what," I say. "You bring this cat home and I'll look him over — see if he's good enough for you. How's that?"

She grabs me around the neck and kisses me. "Oh Mack!" Ronnie comes in again. He be wanting to kiss me too soon the way things going. Oh yeah. "I shouldn't say it, but I — I *know* you'll like him."

"Who?" Ronnie says.

"You babes," I say.

"Me?"

Selma laughs and we all go into the living room, watch sweet Floyd and his wife gas with America.

After a while everybody eating cake and coffee and kissing everybody good night. Family of the year, that's us. I tell Ronnie I meet him in the schoolyard next morning — up in Central Park, near the baseball fields, where Willa lives — and then I move out. Mr. Rubin, he's standing out in front. "How's Julie?" I ask. "Not so good," he says. "Why don't you stop by some time?"

"Sure," I say.

"Look, Mack," he says. "Julie, he still idolizes you. I know it. It would mean something to him."

"Sure," I say.

"If he's well, Mrs. Rubin and I, we're hoping to take him out again next week — if the doctor says yes, maybe even to your game — "

"See you, Mr. Rubin." I get to the corner I look around, see if I still got somebody tailing me. I get whoever it is, I give it to him good. At Willa's, I see a light on under the door. How come? She's usually not home for another hour.

"Come on in, Mack honey — " I hear. It's a guy's voice. I step inside and this guy, about my age, he's sitting in the rocking chair, holding Willie, giving him his bottle. Next to him, standing by the crib, is this white guy, filing his nails. The guy in the chair, he's wearing sharp clothes, a sport jacket with a silk tie, his hair slicked back, he smiles at me I see he got a broken front tooth. "Bet you don't remember who I am — " he says. "C'mon, guess — " He stands up and gives the baby to the other guy, comes toward me, hand out. "Nat Morgan, Mack. You remember me?"

He's about my height, maybe an inch shorter, got a bull neck. I shake hands. "What you want?"

"Just came to have a friendly chat — me and Frankie here." He laughs and his stooge laughs too. The stooge, he looks like these guys you see at the Garden, wearing an old suit too big for them, without a tie, but with the top button of his shirt closed. Every few seconds his shoulders twitch, and he got black greasy hair, combed back into a d.a. Keeps blinking his eyes. "Word gets around, Mack, and I heard about you and me playing against each other next week. How about that?"

"How about what?"

"So I said to myself, Nat baby, it's time you and Mack got together — two former stars like us. Huh? I mean, like you and me, we're in the same boat, Mack. You know what I mean?"

"No."

Morgan laughs. He looks at Frankie. "Mack — he got a sense of humor, huh?" Frankie just blinks.

"How'd you get your ass in here, Morgan?" I say.

Morgan sits down again, cracks his knuckles. "Oh man," he says. "What you think? You the first guy to ever get a key to this apartment? Say — crazy Willa, she still working down at that restaurant?"

"You," I say to Frankie. "You put little Willie down, hear? Then both of you get your butts out of here. Got it?"

"Don't get so tough, huh Mack? Shit!" He smiles, slow, like he's dreaming. "C'mon, huh? Why you got to get sore at me? I just come here to be friendly, wish

you luck in next week's game. Shit! Gimme a cigarette, Frankie, and put that dumb kid in his crib."
Frankie, he moves quick when Morgan talks. Don't
open his mouth, though. I size him up. He ain't big,
but he got the broad neck too. I'd have to go some to
take care of the two of them. Morgan, he draws in on
the cigarette and relaxes. "How bout you, Mack?
Frankie — give Mack here a cigarette, huh?"

"Keep it," I say. I step back, look around. In the
closet, crazy Willa, she got a baseball bat.

"What's the matter, you in training?"

"Yeah," I say.

"We'll see about that next week. You want to put a
little bet on the game, maybe? How bout getting your
guys together — say, ten bucks a man, with you and
me laying down twenty-five each additional. A side
bet, huh? For old time's sake —"

"I'll let you know," I say.

"Sure," he says. Then he leans forward. "You're
okay, Mack," he says. "I mean, nobody's gonna get
you to say anything or do anything you don't want,
huh?"

"You got something to say, Morgan, say it — otherwise I'll see you next week."

"See," Morgan says to Frankie. "Ain't he like I said?
I remember you from the D. A.'s office, Mack. They
couldn't get dick out of you — everybody else, they
were scared green, but not you. They couldn't touch
you. How you been —? I mean, how you been making
it the last five years? That's a sharp jacket you got
on. I hear you got a real high-class job now —" I take

a step toward the closet, Frankie, he stops filing his nails, blinks at me, Morgan, back to me. Dumb Willie, he starts crying. I walk over to the crib, shove Frankie out of the way. Dumb Willie, he see me, he stop crying, reaches up his two fat arms and I pick him up. "Ain't that sweet?" Morgan says. "Last time I seen that kid, he was as dumb as he is now. He gonna be like you someday — only I bet he *never* gonna open his mouth to say anything." He drags some more on his cigarette. "Sure you don't want a light, Mack?" I give little Willie his bottle and lay him down. Morgan, he's out of his chair, walking around the room. The mother got long arms, about to his knees. Big fucking hands. "It's this way, Mack. Word gets around about how you burning things up in our league — I mean, you and me, we're superstars, huh? — and I got to thinking that you might be our man, me and Frankie. What you think?"

"Don't know what you're talking about, Morgan."

"Yeah," he says. He comes up to me and looks in my eyes, quick, then goes by, keeps talking. "Rocks like us, we got to stick together, you know what I mean?" He turns his back to me, looks at Frankie and sits down again. "So I asked around and found out about your job and I say to myself, Mack and me, we like brothers, see — getting screwed the same way cause of the fixes, both coming from Brooklyn, and both ending up playing in the same league. We like brothers. I mean, we got screwed out of making good money, right?" I move over to the closet. Frankie, he keeps his eyes on me. "Right, Frankie?" Frankie don't say nothing. "And you and Willa — that gives us something else we got in common, you know?" He laughs easy, then stops. "So I say, how about cutting Mack in for some big money. He deserves it. Yeah. Look — you make it good like me, you get your own private helper, like Frankie, go everywhere with you, even wipe your ass, you ask him to. Right, Frankie?" Frankie, he blinks a couple of times, but don't say nothing. "So what you say, Mack?"

"About what?"

"Oh man," he says. "What you want from me? Blood, honey? How much more I got to spell out for you?" He looks over at Frankie again, then shifts in the rocking chair. "C'mon!" he orders Frankie. Frankie lights him another cigarette, but he does it slow, real slow. "Okay," he says and Frankie reaches into his pocket, brings out a few brown envelopes, gives them to Morgan. "Good money in these," he says. Then he leans forward. "We got peanuts here, see? Nickel, dime, quarter bags — half for you, half for us — okay?"

"Okay what?"

He gets up. "C'mon," he says, tough now. "Don't dick around with me, huh? I'm trying to put you on to something good. Free stuff, too, honey. You don't want to use it yourself, you get all the profits. Me, I'm doing okay. Right, Frankie? I play it smart." Frankie just keeps filing those nails. I keep my eye on him. I think: I can stall till Willa gets here, we take on both of them. Willa, she's a slugger. "Look," Morgan says. "You don't got to say nothing. You got my message, right, man? You think it over and we talk again next week, okay? How's that sound?"

"Sure," I say. "Don't forget to bring your sneakers."

Morgan laughs and goes over to Frankie, hanging on his back. "See —" he says. "I told you Mack was our man. Shit! You can do okay, Mack. We need another good man in Brooklyn, see. You got a good name, people know you —" He comes over to me, scratches his chin. He got a moustache, trimmed thin and even like Sugar Ray. He sniffs like a boxer too, then rubs his nose with the back of his hand. I open the door. "Tell you something else, you do okay, maybe we put your brother to work too — where he goes to school we —" I got him hung up on the door, gonna bash his ugly face in. Frankie, he's got my arms pressed, though. How he get to me so quick?

"Hey, Mack," Morgan says, laughing easy. "What you want to fight with me for, huh, man? I mean, I'm just trying to help you, don't you see? You and me, like I say, we're in the same boat. Why you want to do anything to me?" He laughs again, straightens his tie. "Anyway, why you want to mess up Willa's apartment? She got it fixed so nice. Yeah. And little Willie, he liable to get hurt, huh Frankie?" Frankie, he press in right over my elbows with power, but if I want I can shake him off, give it to Morgan good, once. "Leave off my brother is all," I say. I give Frankie an elbow and he backs off. Up close, Morgan, he smells sweet, like he's chewing Sen-Sens. "Sure, Mack," he says. "But you think it over, huh? You don't got to say nothing — you don't want to make

some easy cash, you just say so and everything's the
way it was. Okay, man? We still friends, huh?" I
look him in the eye, hard, but he just smiles like he
knows it all and motions to Frankie, then goes into
the hall, leans against the bannister. "You think it
over, Mack. About the money on the game too. Me
and my boys — you gotta watch us. We're tough,
you know? You think it over." He looks at Frankie.
"Good seeing you, Mack honey. You give my love
to crazy Willa, huh?"

"Morgan," I say. "You born dumb, you gonna die
the same way."

Frankie, I get a rise out of him, first time. He looks
at me and don't blink. Morgan, he just laughs. "Sure,"
Morgan says. "And you the one got the real good
job. You really making it, Mack!" He starts to say
something else to me, but changes his mind and heads
down the stairs. "C'mon," he says to Frankie. "You
and me, honey, we gotta stick together, Mack. Remember —" Frankie, he turns and looks at me again,
I spit. Then he nods his head once at me, and smiles
slow, twitching his shoulders. "I see you again, you
better walk the other way," I say and slam the door.
I hear him go down the stairs after Morgan, slow.

Morgan, I get him alone, I kill him, the dumb fuck.
Man, you got to be real dumb, get mixed up pushing
that stuff. I think: he making it so big, he such a
hotshot, how come he playing in this rinky-dink
league? I go over to Willie, lift him up, bounce his
stomach on the top of my head the way he likes. "Hey,
Willie, what's going on, babe? You think all these

months it's been Morgan trailing me, huh? What you think?" Willie, he giggles. I look at him, bend my head back. How come he so happy? All you got to do is bounce him, he smiles big. Willa comes home, she's tired. All these college kids home between semesters, they run her ass ragged.

"You had company before," I say.

"Who?"

"Nat Morgan."

"What he want?" She sitting down, rubbing her feet.

"Says he wanted to talk to me —"

"That boy is bad news," she says.

"Next week's game, he's playing against us."

"Hey!" she says, her eyes bright. "I like to see that, you against Morgan. One thing you got to say for him, on a court, he's the best. You and him, babes —"

"How come you give him a key to this place?"

"He tell you that?"

"That's right."

"He's full of it, then."

"Look —" I say, standing over her. "How else he get in here, him and his spook Frankie?"

She laughs, keeps rubbing her feet. "He still got that cat paying his bills?"

"I ask you something," I say. "How come you give him a key —?"

"I didn't." She stands up, pokes me in the chest. "You want to believe me, you believe me. You don't, that's your problem, boy. Why would I lie to you?"

"You knew him, right?"

"Sure," she says. "Everybody knows Nat Morgan! Don't you know Nat Morgan?" She comes around back of me, locks her hands round my waist. I get loose. "Hey, somebody hurt your feelings, Mack baby? Poor Mack. Bet you want to know some other things too, huh? C'mon, Mack honey, ask Willa and she tell you. C'mon, babes, what your dumbass mind want to know about me and Morgan?" She sighs. "Poor Mack, when you gonna grow up? Willie — when you think Mack gonna grow up, be as smart as you? See? Willie, he don't ask me no questions, I don't got to tell him things that hurt him." She leans over the crib, whispers. "Hey, Willie love, uncle Mack take good care of you, huh? What you dreaming about in your beautiful head? You got sweet dreams, Willie? What you think — you think Mack gonna leave us now that we hurt his feelings?" She gets up, hands on hips, and yells, loud as hell. "Man, you ain't just dumb, you ignorant!"

"Hey," I say. "Keep it down."

"Hey shit," she says. She comes over to me, pushes me back against the window. "I don't give a damn, the whole neighborhood hears." She pulls up the window, shouts right into the street. "I repeat: You ain't just dumb, you ignorant!" She slams it shut. "Oh man," she says, turning around. "How long you think this gonna go on? What you think, because you throw in a few bucks you got squatter's rights here? You got a contract or something? Man, I don't come with a reserve clause. Ha! Look, buddy, let me straighten you out. You want to know why I got hung up on

Morgan, okay. Cause I just *love* basketball players!
How's that, huh? You can put a big six-foot exclama-
tion point at the end of that sentence. Yeah. You don't
know all the Willas there is. There's so many even
I got trouble keeping track, and one of them messed
around with Morgan, one of them's hung up on you.
The others, they go their ways. You want the truth,
I like this Willa about best of all, the other one, don't
like her much, but buddy, you want to pound a punching bag, don't come here. Hear?"

She gives my ear a twist and walks away. What
I gonna say?

"You don't watch out, I give something else a twist,
you not looking." She laughs loud. "Oh yeah, give
him the old Indian wrist burn. How you like that?
Tell you what, though, babes, I got an idea. I do you
a favor, make you a deal. Next week's game, you
let me play and I'll let you stay here. How's that?
I play, you stay. Okay, man?"

"Okay," I say.

She comes over to me quick. "You mean it?" she
says. "I play and you stay?"

"Yeah," I say.

She throws her arms around me, just like Selma.
"Oh Nathan Morgan, you done some good after all
these years — you'll see, Mack, I'll help the team.
I'm no gunner. I shoot too much, you just say the
word. On the court, you're the boss." She got her
arms locked around my waist now. "Hey, you still
mad, boss?" she asks.

"I wasn't mad."

She laughs, squeezes hard. "Sure not," she says. "We gonna practice tomorrow? I got to work on my hook shot. We gonna practice?"

I tell her about working out with Ronnie and she pretty happy. She pours out some milk and we sit and drink. I been thinking a lot.

"Selma, she asked about you, when she's gonna meet you."

"So?"

"So, how bout coming home sometime?"

"No thanks, buddy."

"Why not?"

"Just no thanks!"

"Why you angry?"

"C'mon," she says. "What I gonna do with Willie, stuff him in my pocket?"

"Leave him downstairs, like always."

"I don't want to."

"Then bring him."

"I don't want to."

"Why not?"

She shrugs, don't look at me. "I don't got to give a reason."

I got the upper hand now. "You really something," I say. "You talking before about how long this gonna go on, hinting at things, then I say come on home and you chicken out."

"So? What you want me to do, huh? Drop over dead cause you decided to ask me home. Lucky me!" She stands up and takes her glass to the sink, rinses it. She turns around. "Man, what you think we are, high

school kids? Your mother get one look at me, I know
what she think. No thanks, buddy. When you go to
your house, you don't take me there, and when you
come to mine you don't bring your mother. Is that
fair?" She turns off the faucet and dries her hands on
a towel, comes back. "Is that fair, boy, huh?" She
goes over to the crib, looks in at Willie. "Willie, Willie,
what's gonna be?" she says. "You ever gonna walk or
talk, huh? Tell Willa what's the matter. Tell mama.
It's just you and me, Willie, just us two Willies. What
you so scared of — big uncle Mack here? You don't
mind him. He don't know how to stay nice, it's not
his fault. He just gotta learn a few things. Oh Willie,
Willie, when —?"

"I don't got to listen to this," I say. "You got something to say to me, say it here, don't go using that
dumbass."

She comes over to me, angry, like she's got worlds
of things to fire at me, but instead, she just shrugs,
tired. "Okay," she says. "What you want, Mack?
What you want from me? I don't feel like fighting
with you no more. Just tell me what you want."

"I don't know," I say.

"You want me to come home with you? That gonna
make you happy?"

I shrug. "I don't care." The room, it's real quiet.

"You want me to give up talking to Willie when
I got things to say to you? You want to know about
Nat Morgan? What, Mack? What you *want?*"

"I don't want anything," I say. "I'm tired."

"Tired shit, you don't want to get serious. But that's

okay. You don't want to be here either. Ah, don't say anything. You want to be here too. Yeah. I feel the same sometimes, if you want the truth. I want you here and I wish you were dead. How's that? Okay. You gonna stay here tonight, babes?"

"Yeah. I'll stay."

"Okay," she says. "Then I'll play. You don't want to sleep with me, you can use the couch. Honest — I don't mind." She stops. "Mack — ?"

"Yeah?"

"You think Willie's ever gonna talk or anything?"

"Yeah."

"Do you really? I mean, you think maybe I should take him to a doctor or something? He's happy as hell, but maybe I'm doing something wrong to him —"

"You gotta get him in the schoolyard," I say. "That's the trick. That's where I started. He can follow in my footsteps."

She leans down, presses her cheek against my head. "Maybe you're right. He follows in your footsteps, he be okay. One thing I got to admit about you: you can walk and talk."

SEVEN

I GET UP in the morning, Willa, she don't look right.
"Good job, huh?" she says, turning around over me.
"Shit!" I say. "What you wanna do that for?"
"Man, I'm gonna play with your team I don't want nobody playing easy against me, feeling sorry for me cause I'm a woman. Anyway, where I work, lotta girls got their hair cut like this. I pierce my ears or something, wear these big rings in them, I'll look sharp."
"You're out of your box," I say.
"C'mon, c'mon," she says, "get your sneakers on, we got practice today, babes. We got a deal, remember? Oh man, wait till you see my hook shot! Okay if we bring Willie?"
"Sure," I say, getting up, put my pants on.
"I been thinking maybe you're right about what you said — we get him in the schoolyard — shazam! — he start walking, talking, dribbling, shooting. How come I didn't think of that before?" She stops. "Mack?"
"Yeah?"
"You really think it'll work?"
"What?"
"What you said — putting him in the schoolyard to make him start doing things —"
"Sure," I say. "Like magic."

"C'mon," she says. "I'm serious. Do you think something's wrong with him or is he just dumb natural or something?"

"How should I know? Stop the questions for a minute, huh? I got to go to the john."

I go out into the hall. The bathroom, it's an old kind, got this tank on top you got to pull the chain when you're through. I come back, we get Willie bundled up in this thing, it's a wonder he can breathe. All you see is his brown fucking face sticking out of this blue silk sack. His snow suit, Willa calls it. Downstairs we get his carriage from Mrs. Fontanez and go over by the Planetarium into Central Park. It's a pretty day. We get inside to where the lake is, got this castle behind it, Willa says it's the weather station where they tell you the temperature from the radio. The schoolyard, it's at the other end of this big circle, got all these baseball fields on it, you can hardly see it. I call it a schoolyard even though there's no school there, but any time you got some baskets with a wire fence around them, man, that's a schoolyard. We get there and Willa she keeps nodding to all these women, some of them in white uniforms, saying "Nice morning, isn't it?" and "What a cute baby you got!" and things like that to everybody. Then we wheel Willie inside. From outside I see Ronnie shooting around at one of the baskets. He looks good. Inside there's lots of little kids running around, and these old men sitting around the place where they pitch horseshoes. Ronnie spots us, he comes running, the ball under his arm.

"Hey, Willa!" he says.

"Hey, Ronnie!" she says back. You can tell they're glad to see each other. Ronnie, though, his smile goes quick. "Shit," he says. "What'd you do to your hair?"

Willa, she turns around again, posing. "Like it?" He shrugs. "Samson here took a carving knife to me while I was sleeping."

"Did you, Mack?" Ronnie asks. "You cut her hair off?"

"Sure."

"Nah," she says, punching Ronnie in the arm. "Boy, you believe anything, don't you? Me — I did it! Gonna be the new backcourt star with *Louie's Leapers*. Just watch my style, man." Then she grabs the ball from Ronnie and dribbles all the way to the far basket, lays it up nice and easy through the hoop. You didn't know, you'd think she was a guy, she's so natural. She grabs the rebound, her back to the basket, and pivots right, hooks that ball in bang! off the backboard. Ronnie, he starts clapping. "Bravo!" he yells, just like a fucken fag. "C'mon," Willa says. "What you stiffs waiting for?" Ronnie takes off and she feeds him a bounce pass for a layup. "You too!" she yells. "Bring Willie!" Then she turns her back to me, goes after the ball. What I gonna do? I wheel Willie over to where they are, park his ass under a tree and push down the brake. Willa, she grabs the ball, fires it at me. "Let's see your stuff, star. Maybe we don't even start you next game. Me and Ronnie, we double-team Morgan." She puts her hands on her hips. "Well?" she says. "What you waiting for? You want the band to play?"

I head for the basket, straight at Willa, about ten

feet away I take off, head for the sky, Willa she jumps out of the way and I got the ball glued to my finger-tips, get over the rim and slam it down through. "Wow!" she says. "Wish I could dunk. If I was a guy your height bet I could dunk easy." Ronnie, he got the ball now, about thirty feet out. He got his jacket off, in a sweatshirt. I take mine off. "A Boryla Bomb!" he yells, shoots the ball two-handed from his chest in this nice easy arc. It comes down and bounces off the back of the rim and out. Willa grabs it. "Go!" she yells. "Don't you know how to follow up your shots, boy? Who's been coaching you?" Ronnie comes in, takes the ball chest high and goes up, his face straining, gets just above the rim and slams the ball down, one-handed.

"Hey, you can dunk too," she says.

"Sure," Ronnie says, winks at her. "It's in the blood, Willa. Natural rhythm! Me and Mack."

Willa howls at this, throws up a short hook shot, lefty, it rolls around and drops in and she howls some more. "Oh man, I got the goods, huh?" she says. "Just wait till next week —" Ronnie laughs, gets in front of me, hands me the ball. "C'mon," he says. "Go around me."

"You trying to make time with my girl?" I ask. "Trying to show off by making me look bad?"

"Maybe," he says, grinning.

"Little boy," I say. "I'm gonna make you eat it."

"Just try," he says. "C'mon, big shot!" He's down low, the way I taught him, his arms stretched out, palms up, wiggling his fingers for a piece of the ball, leaning forward on his toes. I fake left, step over right, take two dribbles, turn my back to the basket and feel Ronnie breathing on me. Got him where I want. I give him a head fake right, then take off left, back to the basket with good speed, man, and I feel my shoulder smash square into his face. I keep going, twist around, lay that ball up underhand, backwards, and Ronnie, he goes flying off, holding his hand over his mouth. "You hurt, boy?" I say, turning to him. "Man, this ain't a game for fairies —"

"I'm okay," Ronnie says. "Anyway, it's my foul — I was moving with you." He sets his jaw at me. "C'mon, try me again." I get the ball out around the edge of the circle. I start dribbling right and pick up speed, switch quick to my left hand and by the time he crosses over I got a half step on him and I plow that ball down into the hoop. "Okay," Ronnie says. "Again."

"Hold it," I say. "You know what you did wrong?"

"I know."

"See?" I say to Willa. "He don't need no coaching from you or me. He knows everything!"

"Okay, okay," he says. "What'd I do wrong? I'm sorry."

I go through the moves again, slow, showing him how he got to guard against me crossing over, keep low, not crossing his legs. Big Ed used to teach me the same way, playing one-on-one for hours, till it got dark. The big mistake you make is to play the ball too much, get your whole body over to one side so you be a dead duck if I switch quick. "Okay, guard me," he says, when I'm done.

"What about me?" Willa says. "I got to get some practice too. You guys been playing all those league games —"

"One minute," Ronnie says. "Just let me put him in his place once. Okay?" He's smiling like he knows something. I hang loose. "C'mon, Sam — c'mon," I say, talking to him. "C'mon, hotshot. Hey little Sambo, what you gonna do?" He don't look at me, looks at the ground instead, holds the ball back, behind his hip. He got his right foot planted, teases me by shifting his left one this way and that, then makes like he's gonna start left, switches right, dribbles twice then goes behind his back swift to the left side, like Cousy, and he's got a half step on me, free. He smiles, goes up left and I reach across, leap up and swat that ball straight down, clean. "Wow!" he says. "How'd you do that?"

"Oh man, did he stuff you, little boy!" Willa laughs.

He blinks. "No kidding, Mack. How'd you do it? I mean, I had you faked out and then boom!"

"You got to keep your eye on me," I say. "I got arms like Plastic Man."

"C'mon, what'd I do wrong?"

"Man, you show too much of that ball! You relaxed after you got by me. What you think I was gonna do — die cause you tricked me? You got to keep going, boy, hide that ball with your body till the last minute, otherwise I let you go by every time, just wait till you start to shoot, and reach across like I did." Big Ed, he taught me that too, how to protect the ball with your body.

"C'mon," Willa says. "Give the ball here. I want to try that — what Ronnie did — dribbling behind your back."

Ronnie gives her the ball and she starts dribbling, tries to go behind her back, but loses control and the ball bounces off her leg. She tries again, still can't do it.

"Get your body sideways when you start to go behind," Ronnie says.

"That's a good move, though," I say to him. "Most guys, they go behind, they lose a step — you gained one —"

"Thanks," he says, real happy, then goes back to coaching Willa. She finally does it, jumps up. "Hey! That's deep, man. I like that. Hey you — Jolly Green Giant — watch this!" She dribbles around, lefty, righty, between her legs, then starts toward the basket right, flips that ball around and catches it on the dead run lefty, dribbles once and goes in for the shot. I grab the rebound, fake like I'm gonna pass off to her and spin around plunge that ball down over my head without looking, then grab onto the rim. I'm feeling good, man. I swing from that rim, ten feet high, scratch under my armpit with my left hand and Ronnie and Willa, they roar. Willa, she gets dumb Willie and shows him, he laughs like hell. "Look at your uncle Mack," she says. "Ain't he something! Oh babes, you've got it. Look, Willie, look at that ape hanging up there." She picks Willie up, brings him over. I pound on my chest and Willie loves it, laughs like hell. I'm hanging onto the rim, looking down on the world, I notice we got a little crowd collected, watching us go — women with carriages and old men. I spy one of them at a bench way back, by the monkey bars, I get mad, like to stretch my arm across the schoolyard and strangle him. He sees I spot him he gets up, starts over to us, newspapers squashed under his arm. I drop down.

"Hello children," he says when he gets to us. "Please. Don't stop playing. I was enjoying watching you. How do you do it? Running around like it was summer." He pulls a jug out of his coat pocket. "Do you want some tea? I have a thermos."

"Who's this cat?" Willa asks, going up to him.

Rosen, he sticks out his hands to her. "Ah, you must be Mack's Willa," he says. "I am so pleased to meet you in person after all the times we have talked on the telephone. I am Benjamin Rosen of the *New York Star*."

Willa, she sticks out her big paw and they pump up and down, then he's bending over the carriage, pinching dumb Willie's cheeks. "And you," he says, coming over to Ronnie and pumping his arm. "You must be Mack's younger brother, the star of Music and Art High School's team. Am I right? You are Ronald. I was observing you — you have the grace of your brother. With time, who knows —?"

"Look," I say. "We're busy, man. You want to watch, go back to the peanut gallery, huh?"

"I'm sorry," he says. He pours some tea into this tin cup and drinks it. "It's so cold! Well. I have good news for you, Mack. For us!"

"You want to have a session with me, Rosen, it's gonna cost you."

"Of course, of course," he says, as if he knew it all along. "I brought an envelope with me. Do you think I wouldn't? Here," he says, setting his thermos down under the backboard. "May I have a shot? I can still show you something." Willa gives him the ball, it matches his stomach. Coat and all he goes back of the foul circle, bends his ass, and floats that ball toward the basket underhand, it don't even reach, he tries it again. "We had a much bigger ball when I played," he says. "That was before there were men like you, before anybody had even heard of a man playing in the pivot. Dutch Dehnert invented pivot play in 1926 in Chattanooga of the American League. Did you know that? By accident. Dehnert, he was with the original Celtics — he and Lapchick and Holman." The ball bangs off the backboard, almost goes in. "Ha! Who else? Johnny Beckman and Pete Barry and Davey Banks and Chris Leonard and crazy "Horse" Haggerty. I followed them one season in their one night stands against local teams. We —"

"Rosen, you want to gas, you go try yourself out on those old ladies, okay? We got better things to do —"

"All right. Come, Mack." We walk over to a bench, I put my jacket on. "How come you knew I'd be here?" I say. "I thought you once told me you weren't tailing me —"

"I'm not," he says. "How did I know? I knew!" He rubs his chin. "How did I know? Let me see — it is your day off from work and it is beautiful weather. I know that Willa is home during the day, so I —"

"Okay," I say. "What's on your mind?"

"Don't you believe me?" he says.

"Sure I believe you," I say, then spit.

"Mack, Mack — why must you be so defensive? Defensive. The way you recovered and blocked your brother's shot — astounding, Mack. Only this Russell — this new boy with the Celtics, only he and a few others can do such things. So. Why am I here? Because I have good news, Mack. Congratulate yourself. We have a lawyer!"

"So?"

"So?" Rosen shakes his head. "We have a lawyer, Mr. Jerrold Cramer, and he believes we definitely have a case." He reaches into a pocket, pulls out these used tissues, then finds what he wants. "I came up with something yesterday that gave me the confidence to retain Mr. Cramer. In the Report of the District Attorney's office of New York for the years 1949 to 1954 there is a section entitled Basketball Scandals. You are a star character there, Mack. Listed as 'uncooperative.' But not so the N.B.A.! The D. A. commends them for their cooperation. Listen!" He reads from this scrap of paper. "In the National Basketball Association *member teams were prohibited from hiring players* who had been involved in the scandals. Do you know what that means, Mack? There is more, of course. But that statement, it proves that there was a blacklist. Cramer is looking into it at this very moment. Now —"

"This is my day off, Rosen," I say, stand up. "I should be getting time and a half, talking to you." He laughs. "All right," he says, looking through his pocket for my envelope. He finds it and hands it to me. "Gardella sued for $300,000; Lanier and Martin for two and a half million — and us, Mack — how much will we sue for?"

"You tell me," I say and walk back to the court. Ronnie tosses me the ball and I throw up a long one-hander. It goes off the rim. "Again!" Ronnie says. "You got the range." I throw it up again and as soon as it leaves my fingertips I know it's good. It drops through without touching anything. Willa yells something at me. I take off my jacket. "Well," Rosen says. "I must go. I had bad news before."

"What?" Ronnie asks.

"Sandy Saddler has abdicated his featherweight title — the poor boy, he is suffering from progressive blindness."

"That's tough," I say. Willa, she heaves the ball at me, I see it coming at the last second and jump aside, it hits Rosen smack on the side of his face, knocks his hat off. Glasses too. Willa and Ronnie run to him. "I'm sorry, Mr. Rosen," Willa says. "I was just trying to get this big idiot here. You all right?"

"Unbreakable lenses!" he exclaims, picking his glasses up. He rubs his cheek. "You are a powerful woman," he says, then laughs. He jabs me with his elbow. "I knew it all the time — didn't I, Mack? What power!"

"Why don't you stay for a while?" Willa says. "Then we can go back to my place, have some lunch together — all of us —"

"Thank you," Rosen says. "Maybe I —" He looks at me and stops. "No. I must visit Sandy, spend some time with him. Perhaps some other time." Then he goes and gets his thermos and newspapers and walks off. Willa, she starts saying how sweet he is, I got to laugh. Sweet my ass. Now that he gives me an idea how much money's in this thing, I see why he keeps after me. Ronnie, he says the same thing. "Wouldn't it be great having a guy like that for a father?" he says. "I mean, you could talk to him — and he could tell you all these stories about the way things were back in the twenties and thirties —"

"Hey, Rosen!" I yell. He's over by the entrance but he hears me. "I got something to show you. Come on back, man." He walks all the way back, stopping to pat these little kids on the head. Oh yeah. He's a real father. "I got something to show you," I say.

Rosen, he eyes me and sighs. "Willa, tell me — does he always smile this much? Ronald, you have lived with him all of your life — has he always been this angry? Before the scandals, did he harbor such hostilities?"

"You got questions, you ask *me*," I say. "That's what you pay me for, remember?" I go over to the carriage and pick dumb Willie up. His eyes open wide and when I bring him over to Rosen he goes for his glasses. "Children, they are fascinated by glasses. Why do you think that is so? The reflections?"

"It's just your big nose," I say. Rosen laughs and holds out his glasses to Willie. "I thought you might want to see some magic."

"Mack!" Willa says.

"What?"

"Cut it out —"

"Why? Don't you want to see dumb Willie walk? Oh yeah. This kid can't do nothing, but I been telling Willa about the schoolyard, how things happen in the schoolyard. Right, Rosen?"

"Mack," Rosen says, "if the girl doesn't want —"

"Doesn't want what?"

"C'mon, Mack," Ronnie says. "Put Willie back and let's play, huh?"

I shove Ronnie away. "You gotta add your two bits, huh? You mind your own business, you live longer, pretty boy." I put dumb Willie down on the concrete. Willa comes over to get him, but I shove her away. "Don't worry," I say. "I won't hurt your precious baby. I just want to let Rosen here be in on the start of a great athlete's career — his first steps." Willie, he gets onto his knees, starts clawing at some dirt in a crack, eating it.

"I don't know what you trying to prove," Willa says, and she shoves me back, scoops up Willie. "I told you before, you ain't dumb, you ignorant. And man, I was right. But you're more than that, buddy. You're sick, babes."

"Children, please!" Rosen says. "What are you saying? My God! Did I provoke all of this by coming down here? Did —"

"It's not your fault," Willa says. "It's just this big jerk. He's so stupid, he don't know —" She waves. "Ah, forget it. Thanks for coming down — and for looking out for Mack. He needs about ten mothers to look out for him, you ask me. You go on and see Sandy. Tell him I remember when he beat Willie Pep."

"Okay," I say, going to Willa. "I'm sorry."

"Sure."

"See?" Rosen says, smiles like a goon. "He apologizes. Accept, Willa. Go!"

"Ah," she says, turning at me, but not looking. "Okay. I —"

I got Willie out of her arms then, running with him across the court, he's screaming like mad. I get him under the other basket and set him down. "Watch your genius!" I yell. Then I pick him up by his hands and the dumb fuck, he stands for about two seconds before he falls on his ass. He just giggles. Willa and Rosen and Ronnie they come running. I bend over, put out my two fingers and dumb Willie grabs them. I lift and he stands up. I back up a step and he moves his fat feet along the ground, snowsuit and all.

"Willie honey!" Willa yells. "Look! Look!" She's on her knees, hugging him. "You done it, Willie love. Oh you beautiful thing, you! You done it!"

"What'd he do?" I say. "I just dragged him."

"Never!" Rosen shouts. "He walked! I saw it!"

There's people all around us now, some little girl
about Willie's size standing next to Willa and staring
at Willie. She puts out her hand to Willie and he tries
to bite it. Willa hits him and he starts crying. Then
she hugs him and he laughs. Next thing you know,
she's half dragging him this way and that across the
basketball court, telling him to move his fat legs.
Willie, he's almost as happy as Willa. She lets go his
hands once or twice, he falls on his ass like somebody
pulled a chair from under him. She keeps backing
up, him holding her thumbs. "Come to mama, baby.
Come to mama. That's it. Oh you beautiful thing.
Come to mama. It's a miracle. I swear to God. Your
uncle Mack was right. I got to admit it, babes. Look,
Mr. Rosen, Ronnie — he's walking. Look!" Ronnie,
he applauds and Rosen does the same. "Bravo!"
Ronnie yells. Oh yeah. He's a queen. This parkie
in his green coat, he walks up and down. "Hey," I yell
to him. "What you staring at? Ain't you ever seen
a kid walk before?" Willa's got dumb Willie in her
arms, hugging him. "Maybe he'll walk without us
holding him soon. What do you think?"

"No doubt about it," Rosen says. "Believe me when
I tell you. I am an authority. I have two children of
my own and more nephews and nieces than I can
count." He squeezes Willie's leg. "There is power
here," he says. "I can tell. I am an authority." Willa,
she throws her other arm around my neck, pulls me
over and kisses me hard. "Oh Mack — you got yours,
huh babe? You thought you were gonna shame me,
show how dumb my Willie is, and you did it. Oh man,

who's this joke on, huh?" She hugs Willie some more and I get loose from her arm. "Look at me," she says. "I'm shaking. How's that?" Rosen whips his coat off, throws it over her shoulders, it's so small it looks like a jacket on her. "I got to sit down," she says. Rosen gets her to a bench.

"You are sweating," he says, and pulls a tissue from his pocket, wipes her forehead. "Let me ask you something. When was the last time you tried to get Willie to walk?" Willie reaches across Willa's shoulders, grabs at Rosen's glasses. Rosen grabs Willie's paw, kisses it. "Ah, such a lovely boy you are, Willie! Some day, some day —"

"I don't know," Willa says, dazed like. She shrugs.

"Did you ever do what Mack did?"

She shrugs. "I don't know," she says again.

"What's the difference?" Ronnie says, sitting down next to Willa, rolling the basketball around in his hands, then dribbling it rat-a-tat-tat on the ground, low.

"I don't know," Willa says.

"Yes," Rosen says. "But when did —?"

"Didn't you hear her?" I say. "She said she don't know!"

"I just don't know," Willa says. "I mean, it's like I'm blank — hey, Mack — you remember me ever trying to get Willie to walk?"

"No."

"I don't know," she says. "Maybe he's been ready to do it for months, but nobody knew. Hey, Willie, you been ready for this, huh? You been waiting for your uncle Mack to get you in the schoolyard? You know what — bet it's my hook shot that did it. He seen me go right and left, he wants to be able to come out here with me when the weather gets better — every day — oh Willie, maybe you can talk too — c'mon — say something. Ma-ma. Say it. Come on, sweet thing. Mama. Ma-ma. You open your mouth like this, then put your fat lips together, say mama. Ma-ma. Come on —" Willie, he opens his mouth, but the only thing that comes out of it is drool. Oh yeah. He's a real genius. "You mad at your mama for not teaching you right? Huh?"

"Willa, you mustn't feel guilty for the past," Rosen says. "It is what I have been —"

"Cool it, Rosen," I say.

Then Rosen he's shaking everybody's hand, Willie's too, saying goodby and looking at me funny. "Sometimes," he says to Ronnie and Willa, "if I didn't know better, I would think I saw a look of murder in Mack's eyes."

"C'mon, man. Move your ass out of here. The show's over."

"See?" he says. "Such anger on the surface — it means even more below." He sighs. "Ah, but maybe when you have your money and are reinstated you will lose this desire for revenge. Do you think so?"

"I answer any more questions, it's gonna cost you."

Rosen laughs. "All right, all right. It's been a pleasure meeting you three. Take good care of Mack — don't put sharp implements in his hands. Ha! And come to see me, Mack. We have things to talk about.

Things —" He takes off and Ronnie and Willa start asking me what he meant about the money and the reinstatement. Oh yeah. He drops his bomb, then leaves me holding it. "Nothing," I say, but they don't buy that, so I tell them about how maybe Rosen and me, we gonna get the N.B.A. for banning me. Ronnie gets excited. "What team you gonna play for if you go back — the Knicks? They could sure use you — Braun and Gallatin and Clifton — they're getting old. You gonna have a choice or you gonna have to get drafted by some team?" I tell him I don't know, I'm tired of answering questions. They don't watch out, I'm gonna charge them too. I tell Willa, unless Willie's improved enough to play with us, we got things to do on the court. Soon, she says. Soon her and Willie gonna take on me and Ronnie. She puts Willie in his carriage and then we shoot around for an hour. Willa and Ronnie, they take me on, beat me 10–8 — how you gonna guard two men? — then Willa gives Willie his bottle and I work with Ronnie, one-on-one. We play a game and he gets hot with his jump shot. I beat him pretty easy, anyway, 10–5, but he's getting better. You got to admit it.

EIGHT

WILLA, all she does now is try to get dumb Willie to walk on his own. Oh yeah. He's gonna be another Jesse Owens, his rate. What I want to know is, how come I'm thinking so much about this game tomorrow night? Oh Mack, when you gonna give up? The way I got this game on my mind, wondering how good Morgan still is, you think we gonna be playing before twenty-thousand people.

Morgan, that mother's gonna turn into another Rosen, he don't watch out. Everywhere I go he's waiting for me, asking me if I wanna make some of his long green. Got his henchman by his side. Home and Willa's he takes to phoning me like Rosen, asking if I thinking it over. Frankie, he just blinks and twitches his shoulders. I go to the subway from Willa's, he's standing next to the newsstand, I come out of Rosen's, go home, he's looking at pictures in front of the Kenmore, I go to work, he drives this big black Buick in, I go over to Holy Cross schoolyard with Ronnie to work out, he's leaning against the fence. Outside he wears shades so I don't see his eyes, and these pointy alligator shoes. You didn't know, you think he blew sax in some jive-bombing crew. Only thing I don't like is being followed. Willa goes to work, I take dumb Willie down to Mrs. Fontanez and then head for Rosen's. He's been after me to see

him before the game and I could use another twenty-
five. I take the BMT over the bridge, my eyes out for
the next car, but I don't see nobody. I get out at
Church Avenue though, turn around, some guy steps
back. I keep going. Maybe now that Rosen's started
this legal stuff they got the F.B.I. or the D.A.'s boys
after me. Soon dumb Willie he be on my ass too.
Rosen, he's real glad to see me. "How's things in
court?" I ask.

"Ah Mack," he says, sitting me down and bringing
me a box of chocolate to eat from. "It is good to see
you in such pleasant humor. The truth — things are
going well. Mr. Cramer has been going through all
the anti-trust cases that have had to do with professional sports and he says that things look encouraging.
But you, Mack. How have you been? In the park
last week, you looked magnificent. Here, sitting across
from me, you look like any other strong young man —
but with —"

"Okay, okay," I say, "What questions you got for
me?"

"You are turning into a regular businessman," he
says. "Efficient."

"Damn right." I say. "I tell you something else,
Pinocchio, I'm not sure I want to go through with
this thing."

I sit back, let this sink in. He smiles at me, slow.
"Would you like some tea?" he asks. "Why don't you
have it the way I have mine, with a little strawberry
jam in it?"

"What questions you got?"

"Still the same Mack," he says. "When will you trust me? When will you not think that everybody's out to take you —"

"C'mon," I say. "You sound like one of your columns —"

"Good," he says, standing. "That is good." I figure I get to him, knocking his columns, but he likes it. "Do you know that they call me the rabbi of the sports world? Ha! My columns, it is why you are here tonight. I have one that I want you to read. All right? While I get my tea, read it, Mack. It's for Thursday's paper — the day after the game. I have prepared it ahead of time —"

"Okay," I say and read it.

GIVE THEM ANOTHER CHANCE!

By Ben Rosen

Recently in this column I had occasion to mention a rumor that had come down to me through the grapevine about anti-trust litigation being instituted against the N. B. A. by several of the boys involved in the 1951–52 betting scandals. Since that item appeared, I've been besieged by inquiries. Everybody wants to know how anti-trust can be applied here.

Then Rosen, he explains like he did to me how they can't have that blacklist, how any team can do what it wants on its own but they get together to do it, they're dead, man. He gasses on about what happened when baseball guys jumped to the Mexican League in '46 and were banned for five years. Happy Chandler, he had to reinstate them, settle out of court too. Rosen, he got the facts.

But something more important happened than the out-of-court settlement. The threat of anti-trust actions — which could have dragged in things such as the draft and the reserve clause — made both players and owners wake up. Remember this: until the Mexican League invaded this side of the Rio Grande, major leaguers had no player representatives, no pension funds, no minimum wage, no grievance procedures, no expense money for spring training. Which of you can remember when Robert Murphy, the former Harvard athlete, organized the Pirates into the American Baseball Guild and had them threaten to go on strike before a game at Forbes Field against the Dodgers?

The Pasqual brothers, who lured men such as Olmo, Klein, Owen, Stephens and Maglie to Mexico, shook the monopolistic timbers of baseball, all right. Will the same thing happen in basketball?

Rosen, he tells the N. B. A., they be smart, they let us play. He says that slave market they run every year, drafting players, shipping them to each other like cattle — basketball gonna mess with us, they lose it all. Oh yeah, Rosen, he thinks slavery's over. He do better, he stop there, only he got to lay it on real thick about how basketball's the only native American sport, shovel up all this Holy Joe stuff again, makes me cry.

Let's look at the human side of this too. Haven't these boys who were in the fixes been punished long enough? When they were at college (and even before) they were given cars, money, girls, tutors, and tuition solely for their talents on the hardwood. The world told them in no uncertain terms that they were neither amateurs nor students. And yet when they discovered this themselves, and did things no more "corrupt" than coaches, alumni, businessmen and educators — everybody suddenly became very self-righteous. It's you and I who made them into ballplayers (and little more!), readers — and it's you and I who took ballplaying away from them.

Only last night I went with my son to our Jewish Center, where I saw two of them — two of the finest cagers to ever come out of this city — playing on amateur teams in a benefit game for a Jewish charity. And both of these boys are Negroes and Christians! Both of them are working hard in the daytime to support themselves and their families — living continuously under the stigma of the fixes, one of them with a prison record. Why have they refused to give up playing? Why, being denied the right to earn livelihoods as professional athletes, were they donating their talents to charity? — I leave these questions with you, readers.

Rosen sees I'm at the bottom, he's breathing down my neck. "Of course it needs to be cut and polished," he says, "but what do you think?"

"It's okay," I say. "But don't get your hopes up — I'm still not saying yes or no."

"Am I pressing you?" he says. "Take your time. Sometimes, I know — sometimes I become so involved in the articles, I forget that maybe reliving these past five years is not pleasant for you. But Mack, listen to me: I bring up the past only to free you from it. Can you understand that? Why should all you boys live with this trivial affair haunting your lives? Why —"

"Enough," I say, getting up. I'm thinking about who's following me. The game, too. Morgan, he's good. "You got my envelope?"

"Of course, of course," he says, gets it. "Button up good, Mack. It was freezing when I went out before."

"Here," I say, patting him on the back and giving him the letter. "I got an envelope for you too this time. Thought you'd be interested in reading it. I got it a couple of days ago."

He laughs. "We have an exchange program, heh?"

"Sure," I say. He opens it and his face goes long. You can see all the wrinkles. I look over his shoulder.

Dear Mr. Davis:

I have tried several times to reach you by telephone, but unsuccessfully. Thus I am writing you this note which I trust you will consider with the utmost care. If you have any respect or feeling at all for my husband, I am requesting that you please stop bothering him. He has a weak heart, and, for many reasons, I fear your association with him is, to say the least, not equal or beneficial. If you do not leave him alone, I may be forced to take more drastic measures.

Yours sincerely,
MRS. SHIRLEY ROSEN

"So I guess this is goodby, champ," I say. "I'm real sorry I been bothering you so much —"

Rosen begins laughing now and keeps going, rocking back and forth, looking at the letter, until tears roll down from under his glasses. "Oh," he says, when he stops, holding his side. "This is marvelous, Mack. Classic. 'Not equal or beneficial' — Ah —"

"I'll see you, man. Real sorry I been a bad influence on you."

"Oh my Shirley," he says, chuckling. "She will never change. The letter is beautiful. *Beautiful!* You had better watch out, Mr. Davis — maybe she will begin calling you every night." He offers the letter back to me, then changes his mind and looks at me. "May I keep it?" he asks.

"Sure," I say. "You read it before you go to sleep."

"Still," he says. "It is nice that she cares about me."

"I'll see you," I say, going out.

"Come back soon! Don't mind what Shirley says — Mrs. Rosen — her bark is worse than her bite." He keeps talking but I head down the stairs for the street. I wait for the elevator, he keeps firing his gas at me. I had enough. That's good about Morgan, though, being a hardworking boy — when he sees Rosen's column, he'll piss green. Oh yeah. We're real hardworking boys, good citizens, us.

I watch my step going out the front door, don't see nobody I recognize. The Parade Grounds a few blocks up, used to play baseball and football there. They got some good teams. Tommy Brown, he was only sixteen when the Dodgers took him. I cross the street, head down Church Avenue. I get to the Dutch Reformed Church at Flatbush Avenue I give a quick glance behind. I think the guy's still on my ass, but

I ain't sure. I got an idea. I head right on Flatbush, go past Erasmus, then up to the Albemarle Theater. Lots of people walking so it's hard to tell, but I turn left in front of the bowling alley, make a few turns on the side streets, and soon I'm on this street behind the Sears, Roebuck parking lot, with just a few houses and lots of trucks. A powerhouse too. The street needs fixing, the curb's all broke up with weeds growing out of the dirt. I whistle so I don't lose my tail, listen for steps. Don't hear none. This big Gas Company sign's staring down. I head into the parking lot, go past a car, then fall flat on the ground, quick like they teach you in the Army — hit the dirt. A minute later I hear footsteps. I got to be sure it ain't a cop or a guard, so I look out from under the car and see a guy come in through the gate, looking this way and that, can't make out his face. Got long legs. He looks all around then shrugs like he figures he lost me and puts his hands in his pockets, starts across the lot my way. I get up in a crouch, ready. On Bedford Avenue the cars whiz by. I wait till he gets past me, size him up. He's tall and skinny, so I got no sweat. I leap out, get him from behind, lock his neck in my arm.

"Okay, motherfucker — what you want?"

He tries to get loose, I put the pressure on and he coughs. For a skinny guy, he's got power. I give him a good one in the kidney and pull tighter. "You got a piece on you? Answer, man!" He shakes his head no. "A blade?" No again. I check. "Now you tell me why you been tailing my ass all this time or I'll leave you a bloody heap here, you hear? Cut your balls off." I spin him around quick, throw him against the car, holding onto him by his collar.

"Hey, Mack," Ronnie says. "Take it easy, huh? I got to play tomorrow night!"

I let go and he straightens up, breathes easy. "What the fuck you doing?"

"Simmer down, huh?" he says. "Boy — your eyes! Good thing you turned me around or I'd be missing the jewels of the kingdom!" He laughs but I don't see nothing funny. He turns his neck around and rubs it. "Wow! What a grip you have! You could have killed me, you know that?"

"What you up to?" I ask, shove him against the car. He shoves back. "Easy, man," he says. "Let me get my wind and I'll tell you. I'm your brother, remember?"

"What you up to?" I say.

"Nothing." He don't look right at me. I jam my arm under his adam's apple, straighten out his face. "C'mon," he says, pushing me away. "Boy, what's with you? Gimme a minute, huh?"

"What you up to?" I say. "Who you working for?"

"Nobody."

"How long you been on my ass?"

He shrugs, starts away. I spin him around. "C'mon, boy," I say. "You answer quick or there be blood here, brother or no brother. Won't nobody know who did the job except you and me —"

"Christ!" he says. "Don't blow a fuse, I said I'll explain it to you, didn't I? Let's not stay here — the fuzz bombs through all the time, checking."

We start walking out toward Bedford Avenue. "Who put you after me? Willa?"

"Nah."

"Rosen? Big Ed?"

"Big Who?" he asks.

"Forget it. You know Nat Morgan?"

"Sure — he was All-City same year as you. He —" I get his arm right over the elbow, put the power on. "Shit!" he screams and whacks my arm with the back of his other hand. "What you trying to prove? That you're the strong man of the circus? I told you nobody put me on your tail. I did it myself."

"Oh yeah?"

"Yeah. You don't believe me, that's your tough luck."

"Don't get wise," I say, punch him in the arm, good, look in his eyes and they glassy. I hurt him. "There goes ten points," he says, rubbing his arm. "You got more bet on the game than I do. Maybe I won't play —"

"We don't need you. Who you think you are — Marques Haynes?"

"Who do you think you are? Man, you're nothing but — ah, forget it. You wouldn't understand anyway." We get over to Snyder Avenue, you smell the bread baking in Ebinger's. It pushes the anger back some. Across the street's the Flatbush Boys' Club, played in their gym too. We go by Erasmus you can see the ropes hanging in the gym through the window. Ronnie looks at me I guess he knows the thoughts

I'm trying not to think. "C'mon," I say. "You ain't got much time."

"For what?"

"Just c'mon! How long you been tailing me?"

He shrugs. I hit him again, knuckles out. He hops in front of me, gets on the other side. "Try this arm for a while," he says. "Look — I'm sorry, okay? I don't know why I been doing it. That's the truth, Mack. I just been doing it, that's all."

"You better do better than that, boy. Who you think I am?"

We walk for a while. "Okay," he says. "I been following you for about half a year — on and off — since the summer."

"How come?"

He shrugs. "Just because."

"How come?"

He lets out a lot of wind. "You really want to know? It's gonna sound stupid — "

"C'mon — "

We past Holy Cross, takes up the whole block almost to Rogers Avenue, lights shining on this statue of Mary. The schoolyard's locked up. "I'm warning you, this is gonna sound stupid — but I was worried about you, that's all."

"Bullshit."

"The way you were acting — I was just worried about you. I don't know why."

"You do better to take care of yourself, boy."

"I'm sorry," he says. "Honest, Mack. I started be-

fore that even, you want the truth — last year, when
school was out — you just seemed in bad shape and
we never talked or anything, so — I dont know — I
just sort of wanted to keep an eye on you in case you
got into trouble or something — " I give it to him in
the arm again. "Honest, Mack! I swear — then, after
you met Willa and you changed, I didn't worry about
you no more — not as much, but I just couldn't stop
following you. I mean, it was like a habit I couldn't
break — "

"Oh yeah. Like the way you jack off every night,
huh?"

"Ah, c'mon — I'm being serious."

"Sure," I say. We get to Nostrand Avenue. "You
going home?"

"I guess so."

"See you, kid. You gonna play tomorrow night?"

"Sure. Listen, Mack, are you mad? I'm sorry.
Honest." He laughs, smiles real big. "You want the
truth, it was interesting following you around — like
a spy movie or something, having to make sure you
didn't see me — "

"It was a real gas."

"You could of killed me before, though — you know
it?"

"Yeah."

"Didn't you recognize me from behind?" he asks.
"From my kinky hair, I mean."

"I'll see you, boy," I say. "Now get lost."

"Ah, c'mon. You gonna stay mad at me forever?"

"Just get lost," I say. "I'm sick of you tagging after me —"

"Sure," he says. "Next thing you know, you'll be strung out like Morgan — that'll be real smart, huh?"

I grab him, shove him against the drugstore window, then spot a cop in front of the bank across the street, let him down. "You mind your own business, you live longer. Hear?"

"Yeah, I hear."

"You keep your mouth shut to Willa too, hear?"

"Yeah," he says, looking down.

"Poor Ronnie," I say. "He's so good and pure, ain't he? He's the biggest cockman in this city. Go on home to mommie, lover." He walks away, don't look back.

In the morning I go to work and all day all anybody talks about is the game. Louie, too. He goes out and buys a bunch of White Castle hamburgers for us. Oh yeah. He's a sport. I get to the gym with Ronnie, both of us carrying our satchels, it's real cold out. Some snow coming down, but not sticking. Willa, she's standing there holding Willie. "I'm ready," she says. "Brought Willie along to cheer us on to victory. Right, Willie love?"

"That moustache is great!" Ronnie says. "Where'd you get it?"

"That's my business, boy. The glue sure smells bad, though."

"Where you gonna change?" I ask.

"What you think I am, stupid? I'm ready to go. You just lead me to the gym, babes. You ready, Willie?" You didn't know, you'd swear she was a jock like us, her hair shaved and that moustache, wearing pants. We go inside and Louie's standing there, gassing with this guy got one of these little hats on. Louie, he introduced us and I introduce Sam Clemens and Willie, tell Louie Willie is our new star, little Willie's our mascot. The guy with the hat on, he shakes my hand with both of his and bullshits me about seeing me play in the Garden once and then we go up and change. The other studs are there already and Smokey got a load on. Louie's nephew, he hangs around, laughing at everything anybody says. I get dressed quick and get out on the court. There's about a hundred people standing around the sideline and a few kids in this little balcony they got on one side of the gym. Louie's over by the scorer's table, writing things down, Willa's out of her coat in a sweat shirt and sweat pants, shooting layups.

"How do I look, babes?" she asks. She fixes her tits. "I got 'em pressed down with a piece of an old sheet I ripped. It takes up the least room. Can you tell?" She tosses me the ball and I pop one in. "You got it, babes!" Then she claps her hand over her mouth. "I better not talk too much."

"Where's Willie?"

"I gave him to Mr. Rosen."

I see Rosen over by the window in back of the scorer's table, holding Willie's hands and walking him up and down. The rest of the guys come out and we take layups. Then Morgan's team comes. They're about half white, half colored, big. The place fills up

some more, mostly high school kids with their broads.
Louie's nephew he keeps going to the sidelines, saying hello to his white meat. Morgan, he comes on the
court, got a sweatshirt and shades on, the only guy on
his team without a uniform. He comes over to me
when I'm near midcourt. "Good to see you again,
Mack," he says, puts out his hand. "You been thinking over my offer?"

"Yeah."

"What's the good word then, honey?"

I look straight into his eyes, but with his shades on
all I see is my reflection. He's running his tongue over
his lips. "You listen and listen good," I say. "You ever
come near me or my brother or Willa again, you gonna
wind up a bloody heap. You hear?"

He laughs. "Look, Mack — why the hard feelings,
boy? I said you don't want to cut yourself in for a good
thing, that's okay with me. We still friends." He looks
over to the sidelines, his Frankie standing there, leaning against a wall, jiggling some coins from one hand
to the other. "Hey — how's Willa been treating you?"

"Don't get wise."

"Hey — touchy, touchy!" He puts his arm around
my shoulder . "We in the same boat, baby, so why you
gotta get mad at me, huh? Some crowd here to see
us play. We're in the big-time, Mack honey. You and
me and the Globetrotters. Say, you keep thinking
about selling those decks, meanwhile how bout our
little bet?"

"It's on. We got eleven men — that's one-ten plus
two bits more, you against me."

"Good, good. You mind if Frankie over there holds the juice?"

"It's okay with me. Hey, Smokey — !"

Smokey comes over, zigzag. "We gonna trim your ass, mother," he says to Morgan.

"Hey there, Step'n Fetchit! How much you score a game?"

"Enough, enough," Smokey says. Up close I see he got gray hairs look purple. His eyes half closed. I tell him to give Morgan the money and he turns his back to the sidelines, reaches into his shorts. "Got our finances all balled up!" he says, then howls, slaps his knee. "You kiss your money goodby with Mack and me gunning, brother."

He goes back to the warmups, Morgan smiles. "Bet he'd be a good customer," he says, then motions to Frankie. He walks on the court, clicking from taps on his shoes and takes the money. "Keep out of my way when I drive," I say, and turn around, get a ball from Ronnie. The whistle blows after a while, I hear it through a fog. What's with you, Mack, I say. I feel like I got a screen around me, nothing outside me's going on. Everything's going too fast. I hear somebody call my name, I look over my shoulder, see something black. I walk over. "Hey, Mack, I brung you luck," the Penguin says, opens and closes his umbrella.

"Thanks."

"You look good out there," he says. "Boy, you'd murder 'em in the pros, you know that?"

"We already got a ball boy," I say.

"Ah, c'mon," he says. "I just come to see you play

— Bev, she didn't feel too good, otherwise she'd come too. I got twenty bet on this game — they got Nat Morgan playing with them, and two guys used to play for St. Francis. That little colored kid looks good, too — number 8. I been watching him. Good moves. You got yourself a game. Hey — remember when we used to go up to the Borscht Belt together, huh?"

I sniff. "I smell it all around," I say.

He looks around at all the young white meat, these babes swinging their little titties to get the guys pants hard, he giggles. "C'mon," he says. "I'm a married man — I could have a daughter almost their age!" Then he whispers. "But I'll tell you, around Garfield's sometimes, it takes a lot of will power. I mean, the way they grow nowadays! It seems for every year I gain, I like the snatch one year younger, you know?"

"Yeah. Just stay out of jail, buddy."

"It's like old times, huh? Me with the umbrella and you out there — listen, after the game, how bout coming back to my place for some coffee and cake?"

The whistle blows. Ronnie's yelling to me to come to the huddle. Louie's walking around the huddle like he owns it, puffing on a cigar, waving to all his fat friends in their suits. Like the guys used to watch us in the mountains. "No, thanks," I say. "I got to go — "

"Maybe we can just cop out together, just you and me — like we used to do at the college. We had some good times then, huh Mack?"

"Yeah," I say. "Sure, Penguin."

I go over to the huddle, they wanna know who's starting. I say me and Ronnie and Johnson, Jim Wilson and Willie. Smokey yells that Willie never played before. "He's a good ballplayer — we'll let you in, don't worry, Smokey. We need somebody good on the bench to plot strategy, you know?"

Then they got the "Star-Spangled Banner" and this other Jewish jazz playing on the phonograph and we gotta stand at attention. Smokey, he scratches his nuts. Louie and this other guy, looks just like him out in the middle of the court, looking more like eggplants than ever. This guy with the round hat makes a speech about this B'nai B'rith stuff and about how Louie and this other guy are credits to their people and communities, just like all us ballplayers. It's really something all us jigs out there entertaining a bunch of Jews. I think the same thing when Rosen points it out in his column. Louie's bowing all over the place and then we're out on the court, five against five and two refs, in official striped black and white shirts, they're ready too, and the ball goes up between me and Morgan and zing! I feel good, man, spring up like Plastic Man and twist around slap that ball straight to Ronnie. He fakes a pass cross-court to Johnson and his man goes for it, Ronnie's right around him, he's home free and we're ahead 2–0. The crowd screams like we their home team.

NINE

I BACK PEDAL on defense. Morgan goes out to the post, they feed the ball to him, he passes off. Ronnie, he's guarding this white guy, played for St. Francis, built like a brick shithouse, gets Ronnie under the boards. The ball comes to Morgan, without looking he whips that pass under to Ronnie's man and it's 2–2. The whistle goes off and Ronnie's guy gets another shot, makes it 3–2.

We come back up our way. Willa, she looks okay, tosses the ball back and forth to Jim Wilson, they weave it around backcourt with Ronnie, get it into the corner to Johnson. He feeds me a bounce pass. "C'mon, fixer," Morgan says in my ear. "C'mon, tough boy. Show me, honey. Show me." Ronnie cuts by me, I fake a pass to him, go up for a jumper and boom! Morgan knocks that ball clean away, one of his men get it. How he got up so high? We drop back on defense.

"Who you think you playing against?" he asks, smiling. He still got his shades on. This guy lets go a long bomb from the outside and I got Morgan boxed out. He tries to shove me too far under, I give him some ass. Johnson's in there too, under the boards, it's clogged, man. The ball goes off the back rim once, twice, then comes out my way, a little over my head. No sweat. I reach way up, pluck that ball out of the air slap! with one hand, lower it into my gut and bend over, protect it. You hear the kids all go oooh! the way I jump. Morgan, he's impressed too. He reaches under, as if he's trying to get a piece of it. "Okay, boy, now we know what we both can do," he says.

I dribble out of trouble, hand off to Wilson. He brings the ball up slow and easy. Willa heads straight at me, then makes she's going left, heads right, Wilson whips the ball to Ronnie, Ronnie tosses it up toward the basket and Willa grabs it, full steam, puts in a soft hook shot, she about creams right there, jumps up and down and lets out a "Whooppee!" shakes her fist at Morgan. He turns around, looks close at her, sees something for the first time. We ahead 5–3. "I'll be dicked," Morgan says, looking at me funny. "Man, you got yourself one crazy girl, I say that." He laughs. "Oh man, I seen it all!"

"Hey," Willa says, dropping back off her man. "How you like my hook shot, Morgan?"

"Yeah," he says.

"Somebody got your tongue, boy?" They weave the ball outside, toss in to Morgan, Willa turns around, double teams him, he gives it out again to number 8 and he pops in a jumper, we all tied 5–5. "Hey Morgan," Willa whispers coming up court. "How come you got a sweat shirt on, huh?"

He looks at her mad, I don't know why. "Up yours," he says. I glance around the ref's got his eye on Wilson, bringing up the ball, I give Morgan a quick rabbit punch. He swings around with his elbows, I pin them to the side, the whistle blows and they call a technical against him, say this gonna be a clean game. Morgan about ready to crap, he's so mad, but he just walks away, glaring at Willa. I pop in the technical and Willa goes to the sideline, throws the ball in. "You watch your ass, Mack," he says, "or you wind up some morning with half of you missing —"

"Words don't cost," I say. Ronnie's got the ball in the corner and he just gotta look at me I know what's on his mind! "Chuck it up, Sam babes —" I say, head under the basket, let Morgan get good position on me, deep, for the rebound. Ronnie lets fly with a soft one-hander, but it never reaches the basket. I watch the arc, give Morgan a little ass so I got room, jump up and just as that ball's about to fall short, I get my fingers under it, lift that sweet thing, guide it off the backboard behind me, we ahead 8–5. The crowd loves it and Johnson and Willa and Wilson all come up court slapping my ass. Ronnie, he just grins big. "What's the score, Morgan?" I ask. I get in front of him, he gives me an elbow, pushes back into position. "What's the score, pusher?"

They pass that ball around good. They're okay. This little colored kid got a pair of hands. Willa don't have the goods to cover number 8 so she switches off to their fifth man, who's no threat, and Wilson takes him. They try to get the ball into Morgan, but every-body's slacking off they can't do it, so Morgan goes into the corner and Ronnie's man takes him into the pivot. Morgan gets the ball now I figure he's gonna give inside, but he don't even bother faking, just takes off, left, I stay with him, then his body's flying toward

the basket, but he got the ball controlled away from
his body, he must stay up in the air a full two seconds,
by the time I get on him that brown thing's spinning
past me swish! and Morgan heads back on defense.
They should of called a foul on Johnson, the way he
bounces into Morgan from behind. Morgan's okay. I
got to admit it.

"Hey, boy," Willa whispers to him. "You got a
golden arm, huh?"

"Play ball," he says. "You'll get yours later — "

"From who, big man? — that stooge Frankie? Me
and Willa," I say, "we take the two of you on anytime,
huh babes?"

"Anytime!" Willa says and she smiles big under her
moustache, slaps my ass as she slides through, trying
to pick off me. "We're real mean, me and Mack!"

Wilson misses a jumper and the ball goes to them,
they come tear-assing down the floor. I feel good,
man! Like that sound — ten guys' sneakers bouncing
hard on that wood, the knock of that ball against the
floor. Up close, you feel the sweat, hear guys huffing
in and out. You watch on TV all the time, you don't
see how fast things go. Under the boards, that's the
best, man. Like that smack! of skin when I bounce a
guy away. Ronnie's guy tries to go by him, he steals
the ball and gets to the middle, me and Johnson flying
either side of him, fast break. Ronnie goes up at the
foul line for a jumper, his man comes to him he feeds
me an easy layup and I stuff that ball down, the crowd
laps it up! We go back and forth like this a while, trad-
ing baskets — loosening up the game. Morgan, I got

to admit it, he's got the stuff. I got no sweat with him under the boards, never did with anybody, but when he's got the ball, man, you gotta have five hands you want to stop him. He glides easy, like a cat, no effort with him, got good change of direction, change of speeds. Real soft touch. Shot for shot, move for move, he's as good as I've seen. But I feel good, loose as a goose, Willa says, and there's no stopping me. First quarter ends, we up by six, 23–17, and I got about fifteen or sixteen of those. The Penguin he comes over, wipes me around with a towel the way he knows I like. I see Rosen standing behind a bunch of girls, his arm around this kid I figure is his son, holding dumb Willie up. He smiles big. Willa, she asks us to all gather round her in a circle, then she reaches under and fixes something, the guys jaws about drop. "Ain't you ever seen a girl put her boob in place?" she asks.

"You mean —?"

"Just play ball, huh?" she says. "You feel something wiggle in your pants, you know you got your mind somewhere else — "

Louie's nephew, he don't know what's coming off. "If we're way ahead, can I get in?" he asks.

"Sure, kid," I say.

We go out again, I tip the ball back to Wilson, he takes it across the ten-second line, gives it to Johnson, back to him, over to Ronnie quick. Ronnie drives left, switches right and goes up, but he's way off balance, forces that shot and the ball goes off the boards. Morgan got good position on me, but I get a piece of that ball, tip it up in the air, Johnson and his man get in the act too and that ball bangs around over our heads till I say enough shit! and get space between me and Morgan, control that ball with my fingertips and tip it soft right into that beautiful net. Nobody gonna reach me when I got that feeling! You put that dime up right now, I could read the date on it. "Hey, Morgan," I say in his ear, "you throwing this game?"

"Don't let it go to your head," he says back. He gets the ball, fakes a drive and just heads straight for the lights, hangs up there after I'm on my way down, flies that ball for the hoop, but it goes around and out and I'm off and running in front of the pack, Ronnie gets the ball out on the side, whips a long football pass down to me, I wait a second, look around left and right like I can't figure why I'm all alone, then when Morgan comes on me a second later I give him the littlest head fake like I'm going up and he falls for it. He's on his way down this time, I go up and ram the ball through one-handed, the crowd roars!

"Hey, man," I say. "That your jockstrap under the basket?"

I hear Rosen over everybody else. "Magnificent!"
"The Globetrotters gonna sign you up tonight," Willa says. "Hey, Morgan — maybe you take your sweat-shirt off, you do better — "

Ronnie's man bulls through, puts in a pretty drive, then we come back, Wilson misses a shot. I got Morgan one-on-one on a fast break, he starts over and before I know it, he switches hands, shovels that ball up underhand lefty and it slips in. He got a three point play. "You gonna play any defense, hot shot?" he asks me, we come back up the court. Willa's puffing, it's lucky her man ain't got speed. I pick for her, she lets fly a long one-hander, it bounces out around the foul line, Johnson knocks three guys away, flips that ball to Wilson. Wilson dribbles around while we get set up. I see what's coming, move to the corner. Next thing you know, Ronnie and Johnson got a double pick set for me, just outside the circle, I'm all alone I go up rest that ball easy on my fingertips and flick my wrist, spin it out. You never see such a beautiful shot. Man, I don't hear nothing but the spin of that ball as it comes down dead-center, splits that net open swish! I know I got it when I get this feeling. I could stay out here all day, popping them in, eight out of ten, just like shooting foul shots. That ball goes through and that net whips around after it, almost gets caught on the rim. It tickles that net, eases through, squeezes those cords open like you know what, babes. "You gonna guard me this game, Morgan? Or you too busy sizing up clients out there?"

I'm feeling good now, play him up tight on defense. "Your friends freezing you out, Ace?" I say when he don't get the ball for a few plays. "How come you playing for such a big-time team?"

"Same reason as you, gunner."

"Me? I play cause I just love to make guys like you look bad, you know? Oh yeah. I just got a natural love of the game — "

We lined up side by side while number 8 shoots a foul shot. Willa's had it, so we got Smokey in there and this the third foul he draws in about two minutes.

"C'mon," Morgan says, leaning against me for rebounds. "This is chicken feed, Mack. You got style — why don't you come play with my team? Not these guys — but guys."

"Morgan," I say. "You'll wind up on a slab in the city morgue. I'll stick to this game for a while."

"Sucker."

The second shot goes up and I move out in front of the basket, snatch that ball as it rolls off left. Before I know it, Morgan got his slimy hands around from the other side, slaps that ball away and stuffs it through, we only ahead by three, 39–36. Ronnie calls a time out and we go over, sit down on the floor.

"Geez, you're great!" the Penguin says to me. "You still got it, Mack. You know that? Even these kids here in the stands, when you get the ball they know they're seeing a ballplayer. They'll remember you, Mack."

"You're out, Smokey," Willa says, pats him on the back. "You played good out there — shook them up!"

"Yeah — you think so?"

I look over at Wilson, he leans back, he's real tired. He's playing as good as I ever seen him. He goes to college, he's gonna be a tough man. He does the job.

"How you feeling, Mack?" Ronnie asks.

"Okay, kid. You?"

"Okay. Boy, I never seen you play this good since — "

"Just play ball and save your breath. You'll need it. They're a tough team. They can run. A little luck, we'd be down by three or four baskets."

"Yeah," he says.

"And pop your jumper more. Don't always try to give it into me. That number 8 stole it twice. You telegraphing too much, boy."

"Yeah," he says. "I'm sorry."

"Don't be sorry. Just shoot more — you got a good jump shot."

The whistle blows and Ronnie's all fired up. "C'mon," he says, slapping everybody's ass. "Let's hang onto this lead." He got his fists clenched. "Let's widen it for the half. There's only two and a half minutes left. C'mon!"

"Wait for the good shot," he yells from the corner when we got the ball in bounds. He passes it to Willa, back to Ronnie, to Wilson over to Johnson. I break for the basket, got a step on Morgan, but Johnson don't see me, gets it back out and around to Willa. She starts right and I see everybody closing in on her. "Over here!" I yell but she keeps going, dumb thing, then just when I see her man reach out to take that ball away she dribbles it behind her back and heads left, leaving her man behind. She starts to go up with a hook left and Morgan leaves me, gets a piece of the shot so it falls smack into my hands alone under the boards. I go up and Morgan comes back, ball side, so I feint the shot and give off to Ronnie. He's clear for a five-foot jumper, banks it in, and we're up by five.

"Whooppee!" Willa yells like a maniac, dancing back up court. "You see me go behind my back, huh? You see?"

"You better watch that fancy stuff," I say to her.

"A half inch more, Morgan would have been gone free — "

"I meant it as a pass, man," she says. "Couldn't you tell?"

"Sure," I say.

"C'mon — cut the gas and play ball — Morgan, he's doing okay against you — "

"He's good."

"You're better," she says. "Maybe if he — ah, he's good too."

They take the ball in again and miss a shot, then we miss one. About thirty seconds left, they stall for the last shot, try to set up Morgan. About ten seconds left, he gets the ball on the high post, turns around faces me. "C'mon, pusher," I say. "Go round me. C'mon, Ace. C'mon — "

He dribbles around to the right corner, slow, everybody shifts, then he steps back and starts moving left. We go fast side by side. In front of the basket, Johnson and Ronnie waiting for him, and Morgan throws a head fake, then goes in the air, headed toward all of us. I go for the ball, Johnson bounces him mid-air, and Ronnie stays low, swiping for the ball as Morgan goes by, but nobody stops him. He twists and zooms at this crazy angle, at the last second he finds that ball, suspended, and man, he lays it up so pretty and soft, stretched out his full length, you think nobody even touched him. I got to go some, I match that shot. Morgan comes down, slaps his hands together, happy. Then the half's over. He throws his arm around my shoulder. "That felt good," he says. "You — you're okay, Mack. Like I say, man, two guys like us, with our style, we oughta be on the same team, you know? You think about it, honey. Hey Willa — you see that shot? I still got it, huh?" He claps his hands, fixes his sunglasses.

"Oh yeah," Willa says. "You got the golden touch, Morgan. Golden arm, too. You got it, buddy." He throws his head back, laughs. His Frankie comes over, throws a jacket around his shoulders and massages his arms. "Hey, you two lovers," Morgan says. "You gonna come out for the second half, or we gonna win by forfeit?"

Then he's gone, laughing. They got this record blasting over the P.A. system already, Al Hibbler singing "Unchained Melody." Al Hibbler, he's black and he's blind, but he got the money rolling in. I look back, see all these guys with their little round hats, shoving their white meat around the floor we been playing on.

We go inside and rest up, we get back and push our way through the crowd, Rosen's waiting for us, holding Willie. Willa, she sneaks by so he don't spot her, but Rosen grabs me, pumps my hand.

"I'd like you to meet my son, Jeffrey," he says. "Jeffrey, this is Mack Davis, the great basketball star."

"Hiya, Mack!" Rosen's son says. I shake his hand and the dumbass, he got stars in his eyes looking up at me. So I can put the ball through the hoop, what's the big deal? Some other kids crowd around, gazing up at me like I'm in the freak show. Then back by the window I see Mr. Rubin and Julie, Julie's head rolling from side to side, his baseball cap on, dressed up in a good suit. When's he gonna die? Ronnie's standing there, looks so pretty in his uniform, got long brown legs almost like a girl, you ask me. I walk over. "How you been, Mr. Rubin?" I say. "Hey, Julie, how much you got bet on the game?"

He don't look up at me, got *Sport* magazine on his tray. "You're playing a fine game," Mr. Rubin says. "I didn't know you played for *Louie's Leapers*. You know, it's a small world, Louie, your employer and I, we went to Commercial High School together — " He shakes his head. "Ach — it changed. It's Alexander Hamilton now."

"Good for you," I say.

"We gotta go," Ronnie says, gives me a dirty look. "The second half's gonna start and we want to warm-up — glad to see you're feeling better, Julie — "

I bend over, real low, look straight into Julie's eyes. "You don't got to worry," I say. "This game ain't fixed." Drool comes out the side of his mouth and his head flops onto his shoulder, his elbow goes out from under him. I shove some kid out of the way, head for the court. Morgan, he's got everybody looking at him, their end of the court, doing tricks. Down on one knee, dribbling that ball this way and that, figure eights around his leg, gawking around the court the way the Globetrotters do. Man, you not gonna get me to play nigger, not even with the Globetrotters. He spins the ball on one finger, switches from one hand to the other, goes around his back, quick, then heads for the basket, mid-air, passes that ball under one leg, lays it up, takes

the rebound, flips it up behind his back but it don't
go in this time. Then he goes to the corner, shoots the
ball way up high, almost touches the ceiling, it swishes
through, the crowd goes wild. He gets the ball, starts
to hand it to some kid, then the kid's shaking Morgan's
hand, the ball's gone over his shoulder to somebody
else and everybody laughs. I know the routine.

The second half starts, number 8 puts in a quick
drive and we only up by one. Over at the scorer's table
they got all these little gold covered statues out, waiting for us. Morgan, he's flying high, man. Comes
down the court singing "Sweet Georgia Brown," makes
a circle all around me, mocking me, but I don't give a
shit. Let everybody laugh. It's who scores the points
that counts. Ronnie passes to me quick behind his
back, I don't fake, just go straight up and over Morgan,
I send that ball toward the hoop, I got the touch.

"Maybe that'll shut you up, Ace," I say.

But Morgan, I see it now, he's turned on, man. I
got him from behind. "Okay, Mack honey," he says.
"You watch this, you watch this." They get the ball
into him, the mother bounces it between my legs, picks
it up the other side and scores. "Wahoo! Oh man," he
cries, then bows to the crowd. "Make you look like a
fool, huh?"

Willa tries to shoot a jump shot, but it's blocked and
number 8's all alone the length of the court, they go
ahead the first time. They put a press on, steal the ball
from Willa, skinny St. Francis scores. I never should
of let her play. I come out to the head of the circle to
help out and drive through, don't care who's in my

way. I feel Morgan hit me, bounce off and when I shoot, he's laying on the floor under me. I'm all alone, but the ball rolls around and drops out, they call me for charging. Morgan gets up, laughs. How I miss that shot? "You getting panicky, boy?" he asks. "Maybe you staying up too late at night, huh?"

My fist wants to move but I'm not dumb enough to go for him. That's what he wants. I'll show him next time. Morgan makes both his shots easy, they're up by five and we call a time out. Everybody's face is hanging.

"I'm sorry," Willa says.

"Forget it," I say.

"Watch out for Morgan," she says. "When he gets like this he can do anything."

"Yeah," I say.

Ronnie's slapping Johnson and Wilson on their shoulders. "How you feeling?" he asks. They say they're okay, I put Smokey back in for Willa. She don't gripe. We come back, bring the ball up. Without the ball I give Morgan a move with one foot right, spin left and I'm all alone, Wilson feeds me up high and we cut the lead to three. I know something now.

"How come you got that sweatshirt on?" I say to him. He just laughs. Ronnie hears me, turns around, takes his eye off his man, he throws up a shot. I start up for the rebound, feel Morgan climb with me and as I get the ball I turn mid-air and get him good in the gut with my elbow. He goes down and rolls over. I fly the ball out to the side to Wilson, got Ronnie streaking the other side and he puts in a pretty drive.

The ref stops the game till Morgan gets his wind back. Frankie comes over to him, whispers something and Morgan shoves him away.

"Okay, mother," he says to me. "That's the way you want to play, you got yourself a game."

But he's through. I know it. All I got to do now is give him a little fake and he falls for it. He's easy. They feed me low post I don't even got to fake, just turn and jump and he don't come anywhere near blocking me. Three minutes and I got eight points, Morgan huffing and puffing to keep up with me. His side of the court, he keeps going — from habit, you ask me. Puts in a lucky drive and a long one-hander. Underneath, though, I'm giving him a going over. He tries to get position, I get him with my elbows, shoulders, knuckles, the refs don't see, there's so many guys underneath. First time all game, I knock his glasses off, get a good look in his eyes. "Morgan, like I say, you born dumb you gonna die the same way, you poor mother —" Number 8 keeps their team together, he got sleek moves, and when the quarter ends we're only up by three, but between me and Morgan it's no contest anymore.

"Boy!" Ronnie says, resting. "Morgan, he just pooped out." Me and Willa, we look at each other. "You sure giving him a working over under the boards," Johnson says.

The centertap, me and Ronnie work a play, he fakes defense, then streaks for the basket and I go up slam that ball over everybody's head, Ronnie's all alone and that lead grows. Morgan, he's stooped over some, pain in his gut. They work the ball around, feed him, I tie him up easy. I control the tap, we come down court and I leave the middle open, Wilson puts in an off-balance shot, one-handed, like Chet Forte. We come back and Morgan gets the ball in the corner. "Okay, star," he says, breathing like a horse. "Stop me this time, honey — " He's so slow I don't have no trouble staying with him when he drives, but I let him think he's by me, then stick my foot out, he goes crash into that floor. "I saw that, number 7," the ref says, pointing his finger at me. The crowd boos. Oh yeah, I'm a hero. Morgan gets up, he's gotta have help. "Gonna get you," he mumbles. He goes to the foul line, he's got trouble keeping his feet in one position, misses both shots. "C'mon, pusher," I say, our half of the court. "What you gonna do to me, huh?" I'm wheeling free and easy. "Give it in here," I say and Smokey feeds me. I show Morgan a piece of the ball right side, spin around left and dunk. He's dead. "Hey, Sam," I say. "Lemme guard your man for a while — you take mine."

"What?"

Ronnie, he's three inches shorter, he takes Morgan into the pivot, scores two easy ones, goes around Morgan like he's standing still. I'm clearing the boards, we're running them ragged, soon we're up by ten, then fifteen points with only a few minutes left. The thing I can't figure is how come Morgan just don't collapse. They take time outs and Frankie he towels him off furious, talks to him, the other guys on his team, they disgusted. You can tell. Along the sideline, some people start leaving, the old men. They having a dance after for the young kids to get dry screws. "Hey, Louie's nephew," I say. "C'mere."

He runs over to me, comes up to my chest. "Can you make a layup?"

"Sure," he says.

I put him in for Wilson and we work a play where he cuts off me, Morgan got to pick him up. I tell him not to be scared and the dumb kid comes through, goes right around Morgan, puts in an easy layup. His friends go wild on the side, and Louie's jumping up and down. I see Julie banging his magazine against the tray.

Number 8 slacks off and double teams me, looks straight into my eye. "You're a real big man, ain't you?" he says, then spits toward the sideline. I move for him, but Johnson stops me, holds me around. Morgan, he staggers around the court, laughing, singing "Sweet Georgia Brown."

Who cares what happens now? The game ends with Ronnie putting in a drive backhanded under the basket, us winning 87–62, then they're making all kinds of announcements. The Penguin got my jacket around my shoulders. "You were great!" he says. "Thirty-eight points! Just like old times, Mack. Hey," he whispers. "What happened to Morgan? I never seen a guy go sour so quick!"

Willa comes over, grabs me on my arm, pinches. "C'mon, hotshot," she says. "You gotta change."

Smokey's yelling about our money and I look around quick for Morgan or Frankie, but they flew the coop.

"Goddamn!" I say. Now the other guys around, holding their little statues and Louie's telling me how proud he is, slipping me a ten spot, but I'm going after Morgan. I knock a couple kids down heading for the locker room, get number 8, slam him so the metal clangs on his locker. "Where they at, mother?"

They got three guys on my back, drag me away. Number 8 spits. "You ain't so good," he says. "First half, Morgan made you look like shit."

"Where's our money?"

Nobody knows. Our guys in the locker room now, everybody's shouting and screaming about stuff, but nobody cares enough to fight and they all wind up shaking hands, telling each other how good they played the game. I look in the john, then in the gym again, but don't see them. They show me Morgan's locker, his clothes still there so I know he's somewhere in the building. I tell Ronnie to keep an eye out for him, Johnson too, keep him there till we get our cash. What you think we play for? Then I tear-ass down the stairs, check out the floors. Below they got all these classrooms with crazy Jewish writing on the boards, but they're all locked. I go up and down in the elevator, check the lobby. Rosen's there with his boy, and they try to stop me, but I push him away, Rosen falls on his ass, I don't wait to see if he's okay. I fling open doors to offices and other rooms, check out the place where they pray.

It's dark except for this light burning up front, so I check the aisles. "Hey you!" this guy says, opening a door back of where they got their stage. "What you want?" He comes up close, I got to laugh, a nigger wearing one of those round hats, carrying a mop. "What you want?" he says. "You better get out of here, I'll call the police. You hear?"

I keep laughing, get out of that place, go upstairs, into this big ballroom with fancy red curtains and tables, then head for the back, walk into this kitchen. I about to go, I hear something. Sound like a baby. I go through the back, there's another staircase, I hear the sound clear now. I look down, on the landing there's Morgan with Frankie, Frankie's slapping his face around the way they do in the movies when they're trying to get somebody to talk. I don't believe it, but Morgan he's crying like a baby, all I hear is him saying "Please, Frankie . . . Please Frankie honey . . ." And Frankie shows him something, puts it back in his pocket, laughs real crazy, then starts slapping shit out of Morgan again. Morgan, all he does is try to cover his face, he grabs at Frankie's legs, on his knees and hangs on. I start down the stairs, Frankie looks up. "Please, honey . . . please . . ." Morgan says. He sees me. "Help me, Mack honey . . . you played good, Mack . . ." He got his glasses off, I see them broke in the corner by the wall, I keep coming. "Where's my money?" I say. "Help me, mother," Morgan says, you can hardly tell what he's saying. Frankie knocks him away with the back of his hand, hard against Morgan's neck. Morgan crawls back. Frankie goes to his pocket, I be careful. He takes out a big roll of bills, twitches his shoulders, then counts off what's coming to me. Morgan grabs my leg, I kick him away. Frankie blinks,

I hear words from him the first time. "You be smart, you can make yourself some of what's here," he says, ruffling his moneyroll like it's a deck of cards. Morgan shaking and whimpering, dumbass. "You want to get in touch with me, you look for this animal." Then he laughs, crazy, like Widmark does. "C'mere, Nat love," he says, Morgan staggers over and Frankie clouts him across the face with the back of his hand, laughs. "You worked him over good the second half," he says to me. "I watched you. Morgan, he's slipping, putting on a disgusting show like he did. Things like that could get us into trouble." He hands me a twenty dollar bill. "Let's say this is for goodwill, okay, Mack? I got my eye on you, you play ball with me, maybe you can replace Morgan here and be my number one man—" Then I let fly, catch his nose flush on my knuckles, the blood comes right away. I'm after him, let my fists move quick as they want, I feel something sharp on my knuckles, see blood there too, but that's okay, I know he ain't gonna eat so good after this. I throw him back on the stairs and when he goes for his pocket, I'm too quick, take his hand, toss that knife down a few flights and kick him where he lives, then crush that hand against a stair. His head starts rolling with the pain and I go at him some more, Morgan behind me, crying and laughing and calling me "Mack honey." I keep mashing, I can't stop, tear his shirt, lift him up against the wall and pound his gut, then let him fall like a sack. I'm breathing hard. I bend over and lift his eyelid up, hear him breathing, he's alive. My knuckles all cut up and his face, you don't recognize it, the job I did. Oh yeah. What I do I do good, huh? I turn around to Morgan, and he slides back on his ass, hands over his face. "You ain't gonna hit me, honey, huh?" "Nah," I say. "We in the same boat, Mack honey," he says. "Right?" "Oh yeah," I say. Then he looks at Frankie, starts laughing, hysterical. "Thanks, Mack baby," he says. "Oh thanks!" He gonna touch me but I don't want the touch of him near me. I spit on him. "Thanks, Mack," he says. "Take his roll, you want it — you got it coming, honey —" I pull it out of his pocket, then let the bills drop over Frankie. He's a mess. I look up, there's the janitor on the next landing, staring down like his eyes gonna come right to us. He sees me see him, he takes off. "You better get out of here," I say to Morgan. "Otherwise you be in trouble." I take off up the stairs, look back down, Morgan crawling on his hands and knees, still in his shorts and sneakers, pushing the money aside, talking to himself, going through Frankie's pockets. He finds what he wants and kisses it, then stands up, gets his balance against the wall and lets go with his foot against Frankie's face. You can hear the sound. Then he's on his knees again, laughing and picking up the long green, and I head up the stairs give out the money and don't answer no questions about the blood on me. Willa, she's gone, Ronnie says, don't want no part of me. We pack up our satchels, head outside, you see the spinner on the cop car through the snow as it pulls around the corner. Upstairs, through the windows of the gym, Al Hibbler's turned on real loud.

TEN

THE THING I can't figure out is how I missed that easy layup. You losing your touch, Mack. "You and me, Mack. You and me," that's what Morgan kept mumbling. I didn't hear him then, but I hear him now. You know it. I go to work and things the same as they was, only no more games. I got to get out of this job, do something else. Oh yeah, my talents, I'm in big demand. Everybody wants a fixer.

I come home Friday night, get inside, I remember Ronnie's game, say I'm sorry if I'm late, but everybody got long faces. Ronnie, he's off his team for playing on *Louie's Leapers*. Somebody squealed on him or something, I don't listen to details, all I know is the P.S.A.L. got him for playing in an outside league. "I'm sorry," I say. My old man and old lady, they look at me like I'm a piece of shit. "Nobody made him play," I say to them.

"Forget it," Ronnie says, trying to make believe he ain't disappointed. "It's not your fault. I knew the rules. Anyway," he says to my old lady. "I can play next year, and I'd rather play with Mack than with these fruity high school kids."

We all sitting around the table, Selma comes in, got a black sheath dress on, she looks good all right, her hair up, these long earrings hanging. "Hi," she says, comes over and kisses me on the forehead.

"You smell pretty good," I say.

"Look at my girl!" my old man says, reaches over and takes her around the waist. She don't mind. She turns around on her heels, gets the OK from my mother. Ronnie whistles.

"Selma's having a special date tonight," my mother says.

"Do I got to wait around?" Ronnie asks, wiping his mouth. "I got a date too."

"Where you going to?" my mother asks.

"The game."

"They gonna go on the court without you?" I ask.

"Guess so," he laughs.

"Let me ask you something," I say. "You got a date with a *girl*?"

"Up yours, buddy," he says to me. "*Ronnie!*" my mother yells, stands up, tries to get at him. Oh yeah, not for my mother teaching us to be somethings I turn out like Morgan, I guess. I got to thank her for a lot.

Selma leaves and Ronnie follows. "How's your job?" my mother asks.

"Great," I say.

"You eat supper?"

"Yeah, I ate," I lie, and follow Ronnie out of the room. I sit down in the living room, my old man puts on the TV. "You gonna watch Six-Gun Playhouse?" I ask.

"You sure is a card, Mack," he says, laughing. Ronnie comes through the room and I look at him. He got a white shirt on, this nice V-neck sweater over it.

"I'm sorry about you getting kicked off the team," I say.

"Forget it," he says. "We only got a couple more games anyway. This way I go out with my chick I'm not so tired after, you know?"

My old man laughs. "He gonna be all right, huh, Mack?"

"Yeah," I say.

"Honest," Ronnie says. "At school I'm a kind of hero with that Sam Clemens stuff and playing in the league on *Louie's Leapers* — like an outlaw or something, you know?"

"Yeah," I say, then he's gone, I hear him say goodby to the old lady. When Selma's Roy comes, she's right out to meet him, her coat all ready, you know she don't want to hang around us. Roy, he shakes hands and smiles glad at everybody, he's dressed like one of them ivy-league fags, button down shirt, striped tie and this three-buttoned charcoal grey suit.

"Say, man," I say, standing over him, got him beat about six inches. "What's that you got under your arm — ?"

"Nothing special," he says. "Just a book to read coming over here on the subway — "

"I know it's a book, man — but what's the *title* on it?"

"We really have to go," Selma says, glares at me.

"Hold on, hold on, sweet stuff," I say. "What's your rush? I'm just trying to strike up an intellectual conversation with your beau here. What's the matter — you ashamed of your brother or something?"

"No," she says, her eyes on fire.

"It's *Pride and Prejudice*," he says. "For a course I'm taking at college. It's an English novel, not really —"

"*Pride and Prejudice*," I say, rub my chin, walk around him the way Morgan gawks around me. "Must be about all us poor niggers, huh? You in Selma's organization that's gonna set us all free?"

"Mack!" she says.

"You gonna set us free, huh?" I say, then reach out and he steps back quick. "What's the matter, boy?" I say. "You scared? I ain't gonna hurt you none. Just wanted to see if this suit you wearing was real, that's all." I rub the suit with my finger and thumb. "Man, how they let you into this building wearing stuff like this?" I take the book from him, put my nose in it. "You mean you really read this stuff? Man, you must be a bright college boy, huh?" My old man laughs and Selma picks up her coat, Roy helps her on with it. "That's my daddy here, case you couldn't tell. He's Selma's daddy too." I whisper: "You moving into a real *fine* family, Roy." My mother comes back in, I give him his book back. He shakes my hand, looks in my eyes. "Nice to have met you, Mack. Selma talks a lot about you."

"Oh yeah," I say. "I'm king of the Minit-wash."

"Nice to have met you, Mr. Davis," he says and my old man nearly trips over his feet, getting out of his chair. "Nice to have met you, Mrs. Davis."

I go ahead of them, open the front door. "Nice to have met *you*," I say and Selma looks at me hard. She kisses my old lady goodby. "I'll try not to be home too late — but don't you wait up —"

She don't look at me, she goes by. I go back through the living room, to my own room. My uniform, it's on the bed, those two statues on the dresser. I got to get out too, put my coat on.

"You sure put that boy in his place," my old man says. I go over to him, feel like smashing his face, do what I did to Frankie, but I don't. "How bout running out getting your old man a bottle, huh?"

"Get it yourself."

"Your father asks you to do something, you do it," my old lady says. I just go by her, slam that door. Slavery's over. Outside, Mr. Rubin's alone, tells me Julie ain't feeling so good. "That's cause he come to see me play," I say and keep going. I'm not through. Oh no. I get up to Willa's, figure I can be alone till she gets back from work, she's home, bending over dumb Willie. I don't see her since the game. "Welcome home," she says. I ask her how come she's home, she tells me feel Willie's forehead. It's burning up. She says the doctor been there, give her medicine, he don't pull out of it by morning, she supposed to call him back, maybe they go to the hospital do these tests on him.

"You want something?" she asks me.

"No," I say, sitting down.

"Then move out, buddy. We don't allow loafers here. Go play with Morgan."

"How'd he get sick?" I ask.

She bends over him, rubs his brown forehead. "At

your game the other night," she says. "Never should have taken him out in the snow. Rosen!" Rosen, he let Willie get away, Willa found him after the game, he was in front of the building digging himself a tunnel in the snow. "Nobody made you play," I say. "Nobody made you bring Willie either."

"I know," she says. "I know. I'm not blaming you. I just don't feel like having you around, that's all."

"That go for good?"

"That's right," she says, breathes. "I'm tired of you coming here when you feel like it. How long you think this go on? I told you, buddy, I ain't a punching bag. What you want?"

"Nothing," I say.

"You want nothing, why you come here — what's this, home for wayward boys or something?" Willie, he starts coughing, raspy, sounds bad.

"He gonna be okay?" I ask.

"Yeah, he'll be okay."

I take a beer out of the refrigerator, she comes, grabs it from me, mad. "I told you, boy — this ain't your home! You want something, you ask."

"Man," I say. "You think you're it tonight, don't you? Just cause dumb Willie's sick don't mean I got to fall over and die for you."

"Ah, you're dumber than Morgan," she says, walks away. "Take what you want." Willie coughs some more and she takes this bottle, got red stuff in it, forces a spoonful down him. He don't look too good. "You know what?" she says. "The thing is I'm just plain *tired* with you," she says. "I don't got energy to take care of two babies. How you like that? I'm just getting plain tired of you hanging your long face on my coatrack anytime you feel. I tell you something, I been thinking about you since the game, what you did to Morgan. You know what your trouble is, buddy? You know? You just feeling *so* sorry for yourself. Poor Mack —!" She laughs, comes over to me, pokes me with Willie's spoon. "How come I'm so dumb, took me all this time to figure that out, huh? Why you think it took me so long, Mack?"

"Up yours."

"C'mon, baby, why you think, huh? You a real good ballplayer, Mack, you know that? You in the pros you be as good as any, but you ain't and you don't like that, do you?"

"I don't give a shit one way or the other."

"Bull!" she says. "Oh Mack, you so dumb, how you live? Poor Mack was in the fixes, huh? Poor Mack. You think the world owes you something, huh? Well, it don't owe you shit, buddy boy. Five years you been moping around cause you got caught. You keep it up, you can spend the next fifty thinking about what might have been — but you ain't taking me along, I tell you that. This is where I get off, buddy. You ride that fixer's train yourself, hear?" She laughs some more, right at me, then stops quick. "Oh Mack babes, when you gonna learn? When you gonna stop waiting for somebody to come give you something and go out and do something yourself —?"

"Sure," I say. "Maybe I can make something of myself, huh? Too bad you didn't come home, I asked you. You and my old lady could of got me scheduled."

"You know it all, don't you?" She stops, her shoulders droop. "Ah, I'm just tired of you. You better get yourself another backcourt man with *Louie's Leapers* next year." Willie makes some noise, that red stuff come spilling out of his mouth along with some other stuff. It turns my stomach. "C'mon," she says. "If you got something to say, say it, otherwise get out! Me and Willie want to be by ourselves."

"Sure," I say, put my coat on. She holding Willie close to herself now, talking about how they got the same names. She don't look as big as she used to. I go out the door I know I never see her again. "Take care of yourself," she says, sounds like she wants me to stay, but I don't give her the satisfaction. I go through that door, down those stairs fast. I figure out: I make thirty-five from the game, an extra twenty from bloody Frankie, ten from Louie, still got the last twenty-five from Rosen, my pay envelope for this week, some more saved at home from what I've been making. I got enough to last me a while, maybe I quit Louie's. I walk down past the museum, this big statue of Teddy Roosevelt, got an Indian on one side, this African jig on the other, it's cold out. Where I gonna go now? I think about what Willa does if dumb Willie go and die. Everybody gonna die — fat Julie, dumb Willie, Morgan, Rosen from his heart, the old man, the old lady, Big Ed — everybody gonna get fixed. I make the grade, there be nobody left to give a shit. I got the golden touch, me — getting Ronnie kicked off his team, Willie sick, who knows what with Julie. Oh yeah. You got to be lucky, get me on your team. What Willa says, though, I can't move it out. Okay, I say, head for the subway again, gonna speak to Rosen. Okay, okay.

I get to his place, he opens the door, I say it the way I been planning to. "Okay, Rosen, you got yourself a boy. I'll go through the whole jazz in the courts. You happy now?"

"Mack!" he exclaims, smiling, real glad to see me.

"Who's that, Ben?" I hear from inside, then I see this woman, with an apron on come to the foyer.

"Mack Davis, I'd like you to meet my wife, Shirley."

She turns her back on me, walks out. What's going on? Rosen's son comes wandering in. "Hiya Mack!" he says.

"I'll see you sometime, Rosen," I say. I got the picture.

"Wait, wait," he says, leading me to the living room by the arm. "Don't mind Shirley. I want to talk to you."

"Just tell me one thing," I say. "Your big plans, what we gonna do about them? I'm ready."

He looks up at me, bites his fat lip. "I'm not so sure," he says. "Jeffrey — go to your room."

"What you mean?"

"It's a long story," he says, "but the short of it is, our legal legs — they knocked them out from under us. Remember that thing in the D.A.'s report about member teams of the N.B.A. being prohibited from hiring you boys? Well, Mr. Cramer went into it and it won't hold up. The passive voice, Mack, did you notice it? The passive voice! 'Member teams were prohibited!' — Who can place responsibility? The league — it denies any blacklist, of course, and the burden of proof is with us. To prove a blacklist — conscious parallelism is the legal term — it would be almost impossible."

"Is he gone yet?" his wife yells.

Rosen laughs. "It's like old times here, heh? But why not? The doctor told her about my heart, it forced the reconciliation — who else would look after me, she said. And Jeffrey, it's important for him to have a father. I want you to believe this, Mack, if it were up to me I would continue with my campaign about you boys — but my managing editor is putting the pressure on to stop." He sighs. "The truth is, there has been no response to my columns. I ask you — isn't that a crime?"

"Yeah."

"You know what it is, Mack? People don't want to remember —" He goes to his desk, gets an envelope and reaches into his wallet. "We'll do like always, heh?"

"Keep your money," I say. "Now you got a family, you need it."

He laughs. "You're a good boy, Mack. I'll tell you something, maybe I was all wrong, getting you involved in my madness. Maybe it would be best if you too tried to forget. Maybe this stirring of the embers is no good. Here, take the money anyway."

"I don't need it."

Mrs. Rosen comes into the room. "Jennifer will be home soon," she says.

I look straight at her. "She married?" I ask.

"Don't be impudent," she says.

"Thanks for your letter, Mrs. Rosen," I say and head for the door. She yells something. Rosen laughs and pats me on the arm. "I'm sorry my scheme didn't work out," he says. "But it was always a chance, a risk. Look — sometimes when Shirley's away, you come by and we'll talk, all right? Let us keep in touch, Mack. Anytime you need me for anything, please call. Please —"

"Yeah. Sure." I step outside. "Your kid want my autograph?"

"Ah," he says. "The old Mack is still there! Keep your sense of humor — we need it. Maybe you meet me at Stillman's some time and we spar, heh?"

I hear him laughing when I head down the stairs. I get outside and I feel somebody on my tail. I step into the front of this store, wait for him to go by, but he's too smart, must of seen me. I got to keep moving. You stop moving, you dead, man. I walk around some, up and down Flatbush Avenue, wind up way down by Ebbets Field, go across the street from Fitzsimmons Bowling Alley and get some coffee in the diner, my insides are cold. I get outside, head for home, somebody still on my tail, you can't fool me. The more I think, the more angry I get. Oh Mack, how dumb can you get? Willa's right. What you think, everybody gonna up and die cause you can't play pro ball?

Okay, okay. I got to do something. I head for Nostrand Avenue, hit a few bars, when I get home everybody's asleep except Selma. I wait up for her, don't
know how much time passes, I'm sitting in my old
man's rocking chair, I hear the door open, hear them
whisper a while, go into her room and wait. Least
I can do for her is not spy on how she loves him up
goodnight. She comes in, gets scared when she flicks
the light on and I'm sitting there. What I gonna say?
I hear my heart thumping the way it used to before
the ref threw that ball up. I hear the crowds, man.
I laugh, remember this game when we supposed to
win by less than six but the other team played so bad
we beat them by eleven, turns out they had guys were
dumping the same game. Rosen, he'd like that story.

"What's so funny?" she says. I don't answer, she
sits down next to me. "You okay?" she asks. "You
look funny." She takes my hand in hers and when I
feel her warm skin, something in me snaps and I feel
tears about to flood her out of that room. I stand
up quick, force them back. "Nothing," I say. "Just
wanted to say I'm sorry about tonight."

She waves her hand at me, stands up and leans
against the dresser, kicks her high heels off. "You!"

"You have a good time?" I ask.

"Mmmm," she says.

"That good?"

"Mmmm."

"Look," I say. "I been thinking. I still got some
credits from when I went to college, right? I been
thinking maybe I could transfer them, you know? So

what I want to know is, see, if I went back, would you — would you help me?"

"Sure, Mack," she says. "Sure." Then she's wanting to hold me close to her, I know it, wants me to break down and cry, but screw her, I don't give her the satisfaction. I tell her we talk about it, we see, and get out of her room quick.

Ah, Mack, I say to myself when I get up in the morning. Who you fooling? Who you trying to kid about going to school? Without them strings the coaches pull, you be lucky to pass beanbag. Selma, I hear her getting up, coming in for breakfast I'm out of that house quick. I look back, see if anybody's on my ass. I walk around, I'm at the schoolyard, lean against the fence, it's not so cold out today, the sun's coming on strong, some high school kids playing three-man ball. I hear them talk, they must be saying there's Mack Davis who was in the fixes. I don't give a shit. It don't stop me. Fat Julie, he'll die, they'll pack his slimy fat into a crate of wood, I don't care if he never speaks to me till then. I got legs, man! Across the street I see some guy walking, looks like Big Ed, but it's not. I figure the thing to do is look up all the old fixers and we get a club going. Oh yeah. Roman and Warner and Roth and Melchiorre and Lane and Beard and Groza and Morgan and me, we all get together, we figure out what to do. We set up our own league.

"Hey, fella — you wanna play?"

"Nah," I say.

"Come on —"

"I got shoes on."

"So what?" the kid laughs. He must be Ronnie's age. "You're a mile bigger than any of us. C'mon —"

"Yeah, I'll play," I say.

I play for a while, mess around with them, we have a good time, then the good ballplayers start coming down, guys play for high school and colleges, Ronnie with them. He asks me how come I'm not working I tell him nobody gonna get me back in that car wash. My hands, they clean enough. He tells me he really didn't know I was at the schoolyard, he don't want me to think he been following me again. The other guys, they all know Ronnie, they shoot the shit with him, the kids I been playing with go to the other court, this the good basket, and we choose up new sides. Me and Ronnie play together with this other kid who's not bad. Oh yeah, man. We back in the big-time. Nobody gonna beat me and Ronnie. We gonna take on all comers.